FORGOTTEN MONSTERS

A FANTASY ACADEMY ROMANCE

DARK FALLS ACADEMY
BOOK FOUR

ANYA J COSGROVE

I am no mother, I am no bride, I am king
- King (Florence + The Machine)

PLAYLIST

King - Florence + The Machine
Bring me to Life - Evanescence
Bring the Night on - Eve 6
Dark Paradise - Lana Del Rey
Stay (Rock Version) - Our Last Night

BROKEN PRINCE

Cole

"By Queen Mab, I've never seen a tear this big," Elk hisses into the darkness.

Warm lights from the tents at our backs flicker in the night, and clouds gather above our heads, the sky streaked with burgundy strips of sunrise. The battlefield is barren, though not for long. On the other side of the plain, the biggest Unseelie portal I've even seen stretches like a crack in the foundations of the realm.

Paul raises his obscurion, blue-tinged shadows dancing upon the majestic blade. "The bigger the tear, the brighter the glory."

I remain silent in the midst of the generals, and my hand twitches over the hilt of my sword. Glory's overrated.

Elk gives me a curt nod. "Ready to die at your command, my prince."

"Try to fight first," I grumble.

His dramatic outburst grates my temper, but he's right. There's never been a tear this big. The King joined us last night for a border inspection. A boost of morale.

This surprise attack means they've learned of his arrival, and they're gunning for him. Unseelie pour out of the rift, a storm of talons, claws, and fangs—and far too many of them. Death wrapped in abomination.

My muscles coil with a sizzle of doom. "They're here to kill the King. Go. Protect him at all costs."

The two soldiers inch closer to me, one of them on each side.

"We're here to protect you, my prince," Paul answers zealously.

I'm half-dead already; they don't understand the stakes. "The King matters more."

Shaking their heads, my men stand by my side.

A low growl simmers at the back of my throat. This conversation costs us precious time. "If we survive this, I'll have your heads for insubordination."

Elk grins at my promise. "You are the future of the Seelie Court. The King said so himself."

Infernal magic spreads over my blade and colors it a beautiful, bittersweet shade of purple. If this is my last battle, I'll use every ounce of her magic and perish with her taste in my mouth.

The first wave of Unseelie swarms around us. They know by now that I'm the biggest threat on the battlefield, all because my late wife left me a seed of infernal magic. It's not half of what she was capable of, but it's enough to make them fear me. My trusted blade sinks into my enemies.

A head rolls at my feet.

Blood splashes my cheeks.

Claws dig into my flesh, but I shrug them off and use the pain to focus, building spikes of magic around me and my men, each of them aimed at the Unseelie's hearts.

I fight one monster after another until my thoughts become still and quiet. The clarity I get in battle is unparalleled.

I've known love.

Played with it and used it recklessly. Pushed and pulled at it to see if it would break.

I haven't been taught to handle things with care. Objects, animals, and people existed to serve me. My family ruled the world. I was meant to make my mark on history and live a fearless life.

Immortality makes you jaded and dauntless, but I knew who I was and what I wanted.

I lost it all when I lost Jules.

Since the wretched day Trent Darkwood delivered her body on my doorstep, I've dreamt of nothing else. I have no need for friends and family, only violence. Vengeance. War spread like wildfire through the realm, so there are enough Unseelie in my kingdom for me to fight until my last breath. Battlefields offer no time for regrets. Swords speak a straight-forward language, and bloodshed soothes broken hearts.

Not everyone deserves a second chance.

1

LAND DOWN UNDER

Jules

Frost skitters across my neck. Allie's grip on my midriff loosens, and I curl into a ball on the rectangular paving stones to examine the sneaky dagger buried deep in my side.

Irregular breaths quake my sister as she leans forward, hands on her thighs, her lips blue from the freeze of inter-realm travel. "Jules! Are you okay? Gods, you're bleeding too much."

The thick red pool on the pavement justifies her claim. Fuck. I never saw Darkwood coming. I was so focused on the tear. He needed the horn, so I didn't think he would kill me before getting it. By some vicious coincidence, he aimed for the exact same spot the Fae archer's arrow hit back in Faerie, when Cole's mother almost managed to get rid of me. My left kidney has seriously bad karma.

Gone are the closely-knit trees of Dark Falls' forest, and I shiver at the chill of this new world. "Where are we?" Half-coagulated blood sticks to my hands.

"An Underworld…castle?" Allie scans the spider-infested hall we invaded.

A vaulted ceiling hangs high above our heads, and a wide archway opens to a dark, stormy sea. Rain barrels along the pavement beyond the arch, a gusty, wet breeze bellowing inside the building.

The portal shrivels behind me and seals itself in one breath. The darkness thickens, and my eyes slowly adjust to the lack of light. Onyx lays unconscious on her side a few feet to my left, claws out, her dark silhouette blending with the surrounding shadows. The perverse taste of death sticks to my tongue, but I'm not as weak as I was a minute ago. A part of my soul stirs to life in this gloomy, barren room. I shuffle to a seated position and force an erratic breath down my lungs. Another wave of blood pours out of my belly, and I grip the hilt of the blade, ready to test my new immortality.

Allie follows my movements. "Open the portal again, and I'll try to fly you out to the infirmary."

"Darkwood will still be waiting on the other side." I grind my teeth together and jerk the dagger out of my abdomen.

"No!" Allie scampers to my side. "Don't pull it out, you'll just bleed more, and I'm no heal—"

Eyes wide as a goblin in a gold mine and face pale as a newborn vampire, Allie inches up my bloody shirt. "You—you're healing."

"It's a long story." I can almost taste Cole's *I told you so* on my tongue. Both for Darkwood's treachery, and the immortality I was ready to spit back in his face. The damn prince was literally proven right *minutes* after our fight, and anger sizzles in my veins at the realization.

Cole's warning pounds in my ears. *Wake up, Jules, you're running blindly into a nest of monsters.*

Despite the size of the dagger, the gash starts to heal. Still hurts like a bitch, though, so I clench my fists and wait. "Give me a minute, and I'll open the portal again."

Allie's arms fall to her sides. "Jules, what the fuck is going on?"

"I'm going to be alright."

She squeezes my hand. "How?"

A large shadow suddenly erupts into the room, but the intruder stops dead in his tracks. A big leather bag hangs under his shoulder. His torch casts a warm light over his chiseled jaw as he unsheathes a blue-tinged dagger with his free hand.

Allie jerks to her feet and spreads her arms wide. Electricity trickles out of her palms. "Stay back."

Blood drains from the stranger's tanned face, giving him a ghastly, sickly glow, and he quickly returns his weapon to its holder. "Hevny ye got brains? Donne use magic in here. Hollows will feel it." His thick Scottish accent jumbles in my ears. He braces his hands on his hips and looks down his nose at us, eyes narrowed to slits. "How did ye get here, lass? Ye better not have touched my Lettie."

The man dashes over to the archway and peeks at the sea. "Where's your boat?"

Beyond the veil of heavy rain, I catch a glimpse of an abandoned harbor. Derelict wooden wharfs suffer the fury of the storm. The white hull of a sailing boat pierces the night—tied at the bottom of the stone staircase, it clashes with the old-fashioned, medieval look of the pier.

The man grips the hilt of his weapon once more. "How did ye get here?"

"We don't know," I lie. We can't exactly tell this mountain of testosterone that we're from another realm.

The ground shakes underneath me, and the vibrations muddle my vision. Everything moves. A window shatters above our heads, and stained glass scatters across the stones with a crystal-clear pitch.

The Scot switches his grip to the strap of his bag. "This storm is no joke. I'll take my leave of ye, lassies, but don't stay here. The whole manor might collapse."

"She's wounded! Help us!" Allie shouts after him.

He wags his large finger. "Nae. Yer friend there smells funny. Good luck." Without so much as another glance, he whistles out into the storm.

Obscurity thickens around us as he takes his leave.

A sharp intake of breath resonates behind me, and I raise the dagger I just dug out of my side into the air as I spin around to face the source of the strange gasp. Where Onyx laid a minute ago, a naked girl crouches on all fours. Her limbs shake, and she stares at her hands, rolling them at the wrist a few times.

Black ink runs over her deep bronze skin, and thick brown waves shield her breasts from view, leaving the curve of her ass on full display.

I scoot closer to the girl. "Onyx?"

"I'm Mallory, but..." Ice-blue eyes fly to the ground, and she crosses her arms over her chest. "Yes."

"You're a girl," Allie breathes.

"Was. Am. I don't—" She presses her lids shut, her forehead wrinkled. "Everything is a blur."

Allie growls at the open sea, hands on her hips. "The Scot left us for dead. I'll try and stop him."

Mallory's head snaps up. "A Scot?" Her gaze latches on the pier, and she crawls to her feet, her knees wobbling. "Where?"

Allie points at the sailing boat in the distance.

"I know him." The girl tiptoes to the arch and leans on one side to hold herself up. "Barron, come back here!" she roars at the night with a melodic, powerful pitch.

I stretch to a standing position, happy to find my legs steady, and brush the sore patch of flesh below my rib cage.

Allie gapes. "Is it because you have the horn on you?" She eyes my clothes suspiciously.

Dust poofs out of the vaulted ceiling, and the vibrations intensify.

"We've got to go." I raise my open palm to the empty spot where the portal vanished. Magic trembles through the air, the power harder to access here than it was over Dark Falls' juiced-up battery. Short breaths quake my chest, and a sting in my stomach forces me to stop.

Blood trickles down my thigh, and I wince. The wound itches, like I've just torn it open again.

"Watch out!" Allie screams.

A massive chunk of the ceiling detaches from the roof above us and careens directly for me. A lightning bolt fractures the air, originating from Allie's hand and dusts the rock into a million tiny pieces. Debris sprinkle my shoulders, and I choke on the dry, acrid taste of stone. Another part of the ceiling barrels to the ground, right where the portal had disappeared. The whiplash of the blast sends me flat to my ass, and the sharp pain in my side dizzies me.

I fail to scramble to my feet and press on the half-healed injury. "Fuck. Fuck. Fuck."

A high-pitched screech echoes from the stairwell just as the Scot and Mallory return, but a large crack now runs through the archway, and a loud, ominous whine scrapes through the building.

"By Hela, yer friends are dense. Hurry, or we'll be hollow fodder." The man packs me as luggage over his large shoulder, my curls cascading down his back. The torch in his other hand warms the skin of my arm. Allie closes the march behind Mallory, her bottom lip tucked between her teeth.

He hauls me to the narrow strip of rocks, toward the sailing boat. I glimpse behind us in time to see part of our refuge crumble. The half-destroyed manor towers against the stormy sky, and purple highlights glaze the thick black clouds.

A chilly wind blows toward the sea, where the dark expanse of water beckons and the torch hisses as it falls into the waves. Icy rain seeps inside my clothes until I'm drenched to the bones. The cold numbs my fingers and arms, though a hot, rash pulse pounds in my belly.

Smoke wafts out of the broken windows of the sailing boat, and the white veil slowly descends upon us. Barron climbs onto the boat, dumps me on the closest seat, and barrels ahead to the cockpit.

"Careful!" Allie shouts at his back.

I raise a hand up. "I'm alright."

Mallory unties the yacht and throws the rope inside. Unbothered by her nakedness, she uses her entire weight to push us off the pier and jumps inside at the last possible moment. My teeth chatter as I shift my legs below me and sit, the white fiberglass under my palms sleek and slippery.

The Scottish sailor maneuvers the mainsail and guides us away from shore—and the hollow-infected manor. The white cloud of hollows hangs thick over the pier, but it doesn't fly past it. Disappointed teeth snap through the air, and an eel-shaped puff of smoke pokes its monstrous skull-head out of the fog, glaring at us before it twists around and whips its tails to return to the fray.

A deep, cleansing breath escapes our new companion. "Hollows hate salted water." He snatches a fist-sized vial from a hidden compartment and casts a spell over the base of the mast. A weather dome sizzles into existence and stretches a few feet out all around the boat. The bubble protects us from the storm, but it doesn't steady the boat, and a vicious wave sends me rolling to the floor.

The Scot wipes his forehead and turns to Allie. "Yer lucky, lass."

Thick with rain, her blond hair clings to her face and neck, almost bronze in the dim light. "You were going to let us die," she says through tight teeth.

Barron pats her shoulder. "Aint' personal. I didn't know ye."

She skirts away like she's been stung and kneels next to me. "Are you okay?"

I nod, but a mix of blood and rain sloshes on the fiberglass, creating a pink, wet trail from where I sit "I need to lie down."

In a daze of pain and adrenaline, my vision blurs, and the wild crashes of the waves flip my stomach.

I'd never heard the term *hollow* before Trent mentioned their existence, but I'd seen one before. In Oz's cabin, the upside-down spell had allowed me to see the one that was preying on Beth's soul. Lydia had seen it, too.

A hollow. A nether being. A soul-sucker.

With the manor behind us in pieces, and a throng of hollows guarding the ruins, how the fuck are we supposed to get back home?

2

WITHOUT A KILT

Allie

Red, blue, and gold scarves hang from the ceiling of the ship's cabin. The interior offers a nice refuge from the cold, but a collection of treasures and trinkets—both magic and fake, if my instincts are right—clutter the space. Three jeweled skulls glare from one corner, an array of parchments and maps tucked underneath them. A tiny bed stretches over the bow, with a bigger one tucked in a nook behind the three stairs leading back to the bridge. Both mattresses hold a collection of colorful pillows and rolled fabrics.

A galley kitchen with a tiny gas stove and a small sink stands across from a table with blue cushions and two narrow benches. Oddly-shaped boxes litter the table and counter.

"What a junkyard," I say with a wince. A vicious wave rocks the yacht, and I brace myself on the carpeted fiberglass wall.

Jules sits on the blue bench and grips the table not to plummet to the floor. "Be nice."

"We should dress your wound," I say as I search the space for a clean towel.

She waves my concerns away. "It should heal itself soon."

I cross my arms. "About that—"

"Need any help?" Barron asks from the top step that leads to the bridge, his arm braced above his head.

"We're fine," I clip, needing him to leave us alone so Jules can explain what the fuck is going on with her.

He flashes me an easy, innocent smile. "I'll just grab some clean clothes, then."

I know better than to smile back. "I'm surprised you can find something clean in that dump."

He pulls his cotton t-shirt over his short, brown hair and throws it into a hamper. Celtic knots snake along his arms and chest, along with Norse runes. The black ink gleams in the faint light, but I quickly look away from his torso. The narrow space puts him barely a few inches away as he changes, and it unnerves me to say the least, but despite his height and hockey-player build, I don't *fear* him.

I clear my throat to disperse the searing heat in my chest. "Do you have matches so we can dry ourselves?" He's a spell caster of some kind, so the request shouldn't surprise him.

"Under the sink." He reaches for a drawer below his bed and strips, flashing me his bare ass.

Holy hell!

He yanks a pair of pants past the kink of his knees. The faded-blue jeans fall low on his hips, below his shredded abs, but the sight knocks the wind out of me for a very non-sexual reason.

"You've been to Earth. Recently." The Earth-made Catalina sailing boat was clue enough that our host was an earthling—or at least shopped there—but it could have been a remnant of his old life, whereas the jeans still have tags on them.

"Aye. The Underworld ain't what it used to be. Earth's nice. Safe. Where else does a lad go for fine wine and women?"

14

"Ugh. I don't need to know what gets your dick hard, Jock."

He stretches a black t-shirt over his defined pecs. "You asked."

"Can you take us back there?" A wave propels me straight into the Scot, and I collide with his chest.

He glides his hands down my arms slowly until he reaches my wrists, shackling them with his big hands on the guise of steadying me. My breath catches in my throat at the intoxicating heat rolling off him.

After a few seconds, he releases me, but the memory of his touch ghosts along my spine. I clear my throat, move closer to the cabin's door, and grab the wall on both sides of the stairs so I don't topple over.

He breezes past me and extends a hand out to my sister. "We haven't been properly introduced. I'm Kayde Barron."

"Jules," she breathes, her palms flat on the kitchen table, her skin a shade greener than it ought to be. She used to get car sick as a kid, so I guess she's in for some pain.

"And I'm Allison." I narrow my eyes at his peculiar behavior and repeat my question. "Can you take us back to Earth, Mr. Barron?"

He straightens the neckline of his fresh shirt. "Maybe I will if ye ask nicely." With that, he whistles back outside.

The nerve!

With a growl, I rummage through the mess under the sink and snatch a few matches from a plastic bag. Jules and I mutter the necessary incantation, and the chill of the rain vanishes. A low hum escapes my lips, and I roll my shoulders back.

The rough tumble of the sea subsides in an instant, and Jules and I exchange a curious glance. Maybe our rude, arrogant host has the power to tame the waves. He looks more likely to spark up a storm, but I can't focus on him right now.

I brace my hands on my hips and stare down my sister. "Alright. How did you heal yourself?"

Her dark blue eyes fly to the ground. "Cole thought Darkwood would double-cross me. He cast a Fae spell to protect me."

"It was powerful enough to last through an inter-realm voyage?"

Static electricity sparks on my arms, and I can't shake the intuition that she's lying. Why doesn't she want me to know the spell they used?

"I guess."

I click my tongue. "You're lying."

Flames dance along her collarbone, the pulse of her anger palpable. "You want to talk about lying? Really?" She rises to her feet. "You go first. Tell me how you forgot to mention you were sleeping with a teacher—how he convinced you to kill an innocent unicorn? Tell me all that, and then I'll tell you how I healed myself."

"Is that a formal Fae deal? Is that something you can do now?" I keep a hard edge to my voice, but inside, I'm shaking. How much of her soul did she sell in exchange for her crown? No power is freely given away, least of all by a man like Cole Desyris. I orbited his life enough to know the prince's rotten obsession for deals and sin. He was not an easily manipulated puppet by any means, and the depravity of his kisses still haunts me.

Jules pokes me in the chest with the match box. "No, it's a fucking promise from your sister. You know, a member of the family you cared about *before* you became a world-class bitch and chose a raging sociopath over us."

Blood drains from my cheeks. "You don't understand. He's not at all what you think he is. Killing Miss Eillis wasn't his idea. He hated every minute of the last few months, having to lie to her. But Darkwood was adamant, and mom was dying—"

She cuts me off, unimpressed. "Regrets don't make it okay."

Judging by her reaction, she already knows about Mom's illness. *How?* I sallow a hard lump at the fire under her skin and the cruel curve of her mouth. If anything, I thought she'd understand my need to protect my mother.

But the gloves are off; I don't care anymore. I sink my index finger in her upper arm. "Darkwood was going to kill Miss Eillis, one way or another. She wasn't innocent, you know. She more than dabbled in forbidden magic and smuggled powerful Magisterium ingredients out of the realm. If we don't bring the horn back to Dark Falls soon, Mom will die. Did Cole keep it?" I ask, my voice laced with fear—and a plea for honesty.

She averts her gaze. "I'm not ready to talk about the horn—or the healing."

"I'm serious, Jules."

"So am I. I don't have it, okay?" Tears flood her eyes.

"Cole kept it, didn't he? You—you married him with no concern for the fallout, but Daniel and I, we're ready to wait. In a few years, the age difference won't matter."

Her already tight jaw clenches in a hard line. "Your *Daniel* kissed me."

My head jerks back as though I've been slapped square in the face, and a heavy, disgusting ball of saliva sticks to the back of my throat.

I hold her gaze, wishing I could leave this forsaken boat. "He must have been trying to coax information out of you. If he thought you were into him—"

"Allie," Jules breathes.

"Do you want me to believe you didn't flirt with him? You batted your eyelashes and smiled so much, he clearly thought he could manipulate you this way. 'Thank you, professor,'" I chime with the distinct timbre of her fake, cajoling voice. "Gods! You practically threw yourself at him."

"Allie," she repeats gently.

I spin around, sink my nails into my scalp, and use my hair as a shield to erase her pity from my peripheral vision.

Jules squeezes my shoulder. "There's nowhere to go. You can't run anymore."

I skirt away from her. Prickly tears stick to the corners of my eye, and I wipe them down discreetly. I lift my chin, summoning the courage to listen to her story. "When did he kiss you?"

"In his cabin. Right before I left. He blew angel dust in my face and interrogated me." She plays with her fingers, hands in her lap.

"He used angel dust on you?"

She nods, eyes cast down.

My stomach flips. "How do you remember?"

"Deveraux had given me a protective spell." The itch from earlier doesn't tingle anymore. She's telling the truth.

A painful hiccup grates my throat. "But you kissed him anyway?"

Her mouth hangs open. "Are you for real? I had to pretend to be under his spell, but it made my skin crawl." A muscle in her cheek ticks before she meets my gaze head-on. "He kissed me and felt me up and said he was looking forward to doing it *again*. Don't you dare imply that I'm to blame. You kissed Cole, too, by the way."

Not in any way that counts, but I'm too shaken to admit it.

Arms crossed, I stare at the mirror at the front of the bow, the cabin's reflection distorted by the shape of the glass. "I need to be alone."

Jules moves behind me. "We're stuck here together."

"Just be silent, then," I clip.

I won't lie to myself and pretend I didn't see the signs. Ever since my dragon took an interest in my sister, I was afraid it would come to this, but I thought I was just being paranoid. I hoped my thoughts were just tainted by my history with Jules, that I just couldn't deal with all the petty sibling jealousy.

But I'd seen Daniel steal glances at her—my dark-haired, fearless, impulsive sister—the most powerful witch in the family.

She didn't have the pedigree for his ambitions, so I figured he'd get over it, but clearly, his appetite for power didn't end with me. "What was his plan? He thought he could marry me, the blue-blood politician dream, and fuck my illegitimate sister on the side?" I chuck out a dark laugh.

Electricity buzzes up and down my arms. Tears sting my eyes, but I won't let them fall. Oh, that dragon has got a storm coming. There are no words to encompass the depths of my humiliation, the wretched taste of his betrayal, but I must admit, I'd felt it coming. Over the last few weeks, I'd slowly come to realize he wasn't telling me the whole truth. His reassurances couldn't soothe my soul anymore, the weight of what we had done pressing harder and harder on my conscience with each passing day.

As it turns out, an assassination, however sanctioned by the high spheres of government, is still murder.

I didn't end up in the Underworld by accident. I didn't trust Darkwood with my sister, accustomed to his schemes, and I grew cold toward Daniel's speeches. As much as it pains me to admit it, I've been a fool. Both men used me for their own benefit. Darkwood is probably using my mother, too.

Did Daniel ever really care for me? Or was I just another piece in his wicked games?

3

CAT WOMAN

Jules

A thunderbolt and a fireball stuck on a small boat...could get messy. Eager to give Allie some privacy, I return to the bridge. She's too emotional right now for us to have a meaningful discussion, and I sort-of want to punch her in the face. She framed Cole for murder and lied to me for *months*. Saving my life counts for something, but it's not enough.

Barron had steered the boat into a narrow bay while we were in the cabin. The change in scenery explains the absence of waves, and my stomach groans in gratitude. The weather bubble still protects us from the torrential rain, though wind blows around it in loud *whooshes* that whistle in my ears.

Next to the folded main sail, Onyx—no, Mallory—chats with our peculiar "savior."

"Lucas and I, we waited for you—but ye'd disappeared—I made a point to return to the castle every once in a while, but I'd lost hope, Mal..."

"I was on Earth, Kay," the beautiful woman sighs. She's perched on her seat with her legs propped beneath her like she's forgotten how to sit.

She looks young, her smooth skin not showing a hint of a wrinkle, but I know better than to assume her age using only her appearance. Dark brown waves frame her feminine features, her eyes draped in shadows, and black ink covers half of her deep brown skin.

The sailor waves in my general direction. "I got that. Your new friends are in a hurry to go back. But you can't travel through the realms without—" he stops as I draw near.

I offer both of them an awkward wave. "Do you remember... everything?" My brain still throbs with the implications of Onyx being a real-life girl.

"It's blurry. When I was the jaguar, I shared its instinct and senses, but it's like I was...lost. Stuck in a body I didn't fully control or understand."

"So, you're not a shifter?" I ask.

She shakes her head. "What about you? How was Faerie? And Cole?" Her face lights up when she breathes the name.

"Does he know about you?" I croak.

"No, but he saved me, and he became a tether for the humanity left in me. When I was with him—or you—I almost felt like a woman again. Everyone else in your realm would flee at my approach." Mallory's ice-blue gaze falls to her lap. "Fear thudded and pulsed through me like fine wine—I couldn't help but prowl on the earthlings...I'm sorry I hurt your friends."

I press my lips together. "Cole was as much to blame as you. You did it to please him." Saying his name out loud wrecks my soul, and tears fill my eyes.

My mind flashes back to the rainbow wine Cole so manipulatively held out of my grasp. How I fought him for it, falling for his charade hook, line, and sinker. He fed me a life-altering potion against my will and spiked my drink without hesitation...and yet his actions *saved* me.

The very fact pours oil on the coals of my anger, because—damn him —he was right. Darkwood didn't deserve my help, and I'm now stuck on a boat in the Underworld. I didn't listen to him, which makes me hate the situation—and myself—even more.

Mallory sighs. "You—you're a Fae princess, now."

My eyes snap up. "How can you tell?" Celeste saw it with one glance. Erron, too. I never understood how, and I didn't want to broadcast my ignorance in front of them.

Allie joins us on the bridge—just barely, sitting on the first step leading to the cabin, her back propped on the open door.

Barron offers us all a beer, the Earth-made drink and Yeti cooler reassuring as fuck. We're not so far from home if he's got Coronas on ice.

Mallory grips the neck of the bottle with a shaky hand. "A tremble of Fae power now surrounds you."

Barron squints at me, and the intensity of his gaze tickles my skin. "If yer a Fae princess, how come you're not all beautiful?"

My forehead creases. "Wow, thanks."

Allie covers a wry but genuine smile with her hand.

"Ye know what I mean."

I wrinkle my nose at the sailor. "I'm not a Fae, am I? I'm just married to one."

He licks his lips, and I feel...naked. His gaze roves over me as though he's asking himself if he'd like to fuck a Fae princess. "Aren't you a wee bit young for marriage?"

"I agree," Allie snaps. Lines appear at the corners of her eyes, as though my trip to Faerie and my marriage to Cole made *me* untrustworthy.

I flip them off in turn.

Barron laughs, the sound gruff and sexual. "I'm messing with ye. I've got no qualm with yer choices. Fae are hot."

Mallory stifles a chuckle with the back of her hand, and long, thick curls bounce around her delicate features. I steal a glance at her tattoos, but they're not Fae alphabet. In fact, I'm pretty sure they're demonic runes.

I graze her forearm. "Love the ink. What do they mean?"

Her mouth curls downward. "It's the curse."

A curse written on her skin...like mine. "A curse?"

With a nod, she tilts her head back and swallows a long swig of beer. "I was cursed to become a shadow of myself whenever I leave this realm."

"Heavy." I rub down my face, but the ache between my brows worsens.

Allie crosses her arms around her chest. "Can you take us back to Dark Falls?"

Barron taps his mouth with his index finger as though he's making some quick, mischievous calculations. "What's in it for me?"

Mallory retreats a few inches in her seat. "Kal...Jules is my friend."

He stares out at the downpour. "Friends or not, I have too many problems to solve and very little time to do it. Lucas is waiting for me in Miami, and Dark Falls is dangerous and well-guarded."

"You're a scavenger, are you not?" Allie says, her curt question sounding like an accusation.

"Treasure hunter?" I offer as a more polished alternative.

Barron's eyes dim. "I'm many things, lass. None of which a babysitter for lost witches."

Allie storms inside the cabin and slams the door behind her. The loud *thump* lances up my spine.

Barron's mouth forms a thin line, but he quickly turns his attention back to Mallory. "And you? How are ye getting rid of that curse? That should be yer priority."

"Kay, we already talked about this. There's nothing to be done."

"I got your stuff. That's why I was in the castle, actually. I heard the structure wasn't sound and checked on your room one last time..." He pats her shoulder.

"Thank you, Kay. You did everything you could."

As intimate and familiar to each other that they seem to be, I get absolutely no romantic vibes from them, which is weird considering both Mallory and the Scot are sexy as fuck. If anything, Barron looks at her as though he was sworn to protect her, like a big brother would, yet their skins and accents are too different for them to be siblings.

"Your emerald pendant. Where did you get it?" he asks.

"It was a gift," I answer. "Why?"

"It's beautifully made." He licks his lips, staring at the heavy emerald between my breasts as though the green stone might break from the chain at any moment. His gaze heats up my gut, as though he can read my thoughts.

"Well…it's not for sale." I clear my throat and focus on Mallory. "What happens if we go back to Earth? You turn back into the cat?"

"Yes, but I don't mind." She angles her face to me. "You took me home, Jules. Thank you."

Something passes between them, and Barron gives her a discreet nod. I'm pretty sure Mallory just signaled him that he should not talk too much about her history—or *condition*—in front of me.

A full-blown headache pounds between my eyes, and I rake my fingers through my curls. "You could take us to Faerie instead, if it's easier."

"No. The only charted tear that leads directly from the Under-world into Faerie crawls with creatures that put the Underworld nightmares to shame. And it's impossible to travel through it by ship anyway," the sailor explains.

Creatures that put nightmares to shame… "Unseelie Fae?"

"Aye."

Ice slithers in my cramped chest. Cole was right about the Unseelie using the Underworld's main channel—an ancient hub of portals—as a springboard for their attacks on his people.

"How long will it take to go back to Earth? If you have pressing business in Miami, that would at least put us in the right realm."

"Five weeks? Six? Depends on the wind."

My lips curl up. "Good thing I took my wind to-go."

He raises a brow in question.

"My sister's element is air." I tilt my chin up to the drop-dead-gorgeous sailor. "I'll make you a deal. If Allie's powers put us ahead of schedule, you will get us home to Dark Falls. If the voyage takes five to six weeks, we'll follow you to Miami and make our way back home from there."

The Scot gives me a solemn nod. "Fair enough."

"Good. I didn't want to hitchhike out of hell."

He opens his mouth to speak, but Mallory grazes his arm. "We'll take you home, Jules. It's the least we can do."

"Buckle up, these waters aren't for the faint-hearted, though I can tell ye're not as high maintenance as yer sister." The devilish glint in Barron's eyes fogs my brain. I swear this man can read my emotions or influence them in some way. Nothing like a Fae glamor would, but his gaze isn't harmless. It makes me want to cower into his heat and spill my secrets, which is totally ridiculous.

With a satisfied nod, I sit on one of the cushioned seats. I can survive a few weeks on a boat. Nevermind that my stomach turned upside-down the second I stepped foot on the yacht, or that the weather in the Underworld seems to be tailor-made to drown out my fire. I'm a reasonable woman. I can be patient.

In theory.

I DUMP my cards face-down on the small table. "I fold."

Mallory raises a brow at Barron. "I raise you my last protein bar."

In the last few days, the demon has adjusted to her human form. She no longer licks her hands in the morning or sniffs her food. The leather jacket she's wearing hugs her forms, and her wild brown mane was tamed into an artsy fishtail braid by Allie.

My sister stares at her cards with a giddy smile. "Let's not play for rations anymore. Let's play for secrets."

Barron sinks back into his seat, his legs spread wide, and rubs the angle of his jaw. "What secrets could you possibly have that would be of any interest to me?"

Allie shrugs. "Aren't you wondering how we ended up in this realm?"

He straightens out his cards with a snicker. "I know who ye are. I figured it out an hour after you stepped on my Lettie."

Lettie, as Barron calls his sailing boat, is a 2004, 40 foot Catalina yacht that is not made to house four people—as he loves to remind us.

His luscious green gaze flicks over to me for a moment before settling back on my sister. "I've never seen her before, but ye...ye look too much lek yer mother."

"You know my mother?" Allie asks flatly.

A stranger wouldn't be able to read the fear on her shadow-freckled face, but I know my sister enough to know she's rattled.

"Nae. But I've glimpsed at the news often enough to know who she is."

The clear innuendo rubs Allie the wrong way because her shoulders stiffen.

She looks down her nose at Barron. "My mother is brilliant and powerful. She's not at all the prissy, pearl-wearing witch *some* media made her out to be."

I bite my lips not to call her bluff. Allie knows how much her mother is downright hated in certain—scratch that, most—spheres of the witches, warlocks, and seer population, and with good reason. She's the epitome of privilege, and being a woman doesn't excuse any of her political ploys or ruthless behavior.

The subject is...sore between us.

Allie and I pretended to be twins in the human world, two stubborn peas in a magical pod. Now, I'm not sure what we are. I still haven't told her about the horn. I can't bring myself to tell her what I truly am. What Cole did. What I've become.

When she finds out the only available remedy for her mother's illness was used to make *me* immortal, she'll hate me.

I just can't let this opportunity to close some of the distance between us pass me by, so I keep my mouth shut and let her defend her mother.

I glance at Barron. "You watch Immortal news today?" I drum my fingers on the table, watching his face closely for tells.

A dark shroud obscures his face. "Not anymore."

Mallory wouldn't tell me a thing about our captain's past, despite my efforts. I've tried to piece together her relationship to the elusive, mysterious Scot, but our host has barely uttered two words about himself. Allie sets him on edge, but he doesn't mind my Fae association. He's a puzzle, and I need to know if we can trust him.

There's not much to do on a boat in the middle of the ocean besides sulk and play cards. Oh, and puke my entrails out. Let's not forget all the puking. I wasn't meant to live on water—it's as simple as that.

Over the last few days, I snooped around *Lettie* and discovered more than one powerful, dangerous artifact buried in the eclectic cabin. Who knows what else he keeps below deck in the hidden compartments I can't open without attracting his attention.

Let's just hope he's really steering us back to our realm.

The Scot peels a card from the top of the deck. "If the Dark Gods had told me I'd be harbouring Robert fucking Winslow's daughters on my boat one day—and not for ransom—I wouldn't have believed them."

Allie and I exchange a heavy glance, and we have a silent conversation. We both hate that he has the upper hand. Ever since we set foot on his boat, Barron seems to know—or guess—everything about us. If only we could learn something tangible about him.

"Ransom? Are you a pirate?" Allie asks with her best aloof tone.

The Scot straightens his cards, his tongue tucked between his front teeth. "It depends...what price could I get for ye?" He appraises her body up and down, and the intensity of his gaze sparks shivers in my body.

Allie's cheeks heat up to the point of turning bright red. She stands up to serve herself another tea, and Barron tracks her every movement.

Mal covers up a budding smile with her hand and leans into my ear. "Allie should decide if she likes pirates, and soon."

With a chuckle, I nod in agreement.

Barron might like to act like he's older and wiser, but I'm not fooled. He's hot for her.

27

4

YATCH FEVER

Allie

Two weeks at sea with rationed food and nasty waves work better than the trendiest diet. After a quick shower, I wrap a loose jacket around my frame and return to the bridge, reluctantly leaving the warmth of the cabin. The mismatched clothes Barron lended me fall haphazardly around my frame. As of right now, we're officially out of shampoo, and my muscles are stiff from the thin mattress and lack of proper pillows.

Jules and I huddle in the nook of the bow each night, while Mallory and Barron sleep in his bed.

Jules is still puking her heart's out over the rails, her stomach wasn't made for sea adventures. At least I can keep in what I eat.

"You look wretched," I taunt her.

She flips me off—not so dehydrated that she can't tell me to fuck off. That's reassuring.

After she empties her stomach one more time, she breezes past me and sits with Barron by the mainsail.

The wind muffles their conversation, but my sister chats him up with an easy smile like he's our new friend. Like he wasn't about to leave us for dead in the Underworld palace with a throng of soul-sucking monsters.

We haven't learned much about our reluctant host since we commandeered his boat other than he's a beast at poker and a bad cook. Mallory keeps her cards close to her chest, too, both literally and figuratively. Jules didn't share her secrets either, our tempestuous relationship at a standstill.

We have a few days left at sea, my powers stirring us in the right direction quicker than Barron had thought possible, the fury of the elements barely hindering our progress thanks to my magic. We haven't caught a glimpse of land, or another boat, since the castle, alone in the immensity of the Underworld's Fallen Sea.

The wind whips my hair forward, and the blond strands snake at the edge of my vision. A dark shadow condenses into solid form in the early morning fog, and I squint at the apparition. The edges of a tall, rocky cliff slowly appear.

Barron bounces to his feet. "By the Dark Gods and their wicked brooms, the Belial canal. It's a new record." He slides under the boom, arms braced above his head, his wondrous gaze skirting the shadows of the outlandish landscape. "You're good at this, little storm."

I grit my teeth together. "Don't call me that."

His eyes gleam with mischief. "Why not? It fits ye, I think."

"Alright, now, we have to become invisible." Mallory dashes out of the cabin with Barron's spell gear in tow.

They warned us that this particular part of the trip could get unpleasant.

Barron motions to me and Jules. "Ye two. In the cabin."

I brace my hand on my hip. "Why do we have to hide? If you expect trouble, we could be useful."

Jules nods in assent.

29

Barron crosses his arms, his gray shirt stretching over his biceps. "Your powers are mostly useless against these creatures."

Ice cramps my chest. What monster is immune to both lightning and fire? "Still, we could help you set up—" I motion to the ritualistic chalk Mallory holds in her hands—"whatever this is."

"Nae. I need ye safe. *In the cabin.*" His pointed glare offers no place for discussion.

I open my mouth to tell him off, but Jules grabs a fist of my jacket.

"He's hiding something. We should remain involved, in case he plans to double-cross us," I whisper in her ear.

She pulls me along. "We will. But this is a perfect opportunity to check what's under his mattress."

I follow her down the stairs.

She yanks the curtains leading to Barron's bed aside and peels the cushions off one by one. A metal latch leads to an inside compartment, and she grins. "Bingo."

The boat hits a huge rock, and I brace myself on the carpeted fiberglass to keep from toppling over. "How are you so calm? At least I can fly away from this raft if we sink."

Jules squints at the ceiling and lets go of the latch. "It wasn't a rock. We didn't hit anything. We were *grabbed.*"

Adrenaline rushes in my veins. "How can you tell?" A shadow crawls over the kitchen porthole, and I jerk away from the sink.

Jules' eyes widen. "They might not have seen that coming. We need to warn them."

A dark form obscures the dim light coming in from the tiny round window once more. Flames swirl on Jules' arms as lightning does on mine, and we erupt onto the bridge, arms stretched on both sides, ready to fry some demons.

Fog clogs the air as monsters curl around the railings. They have human faces and arms, but snake tails below the waist. They stand at our approach, their wide tails supporting their weight.

Black and gold scales luster in the morning light as one of the snake-men slithers toward Jules and me.

Lightning bolts crackle in my hands, and I hurl them at the demon.

His skin emits a low *tsk* on impact. The scent of burnt flesh pervades the air, but other than that, the snake-man seems unbothered by the high-voltage. He raises a three-pronged spear over his shoulder.

I bolt into the air, trying to draw his fire. The sudden motion spooks him, my sister's existence all but forgotten.

That's right. Look at me, snakey.

I dash out of the way of his pointy trident.

Jules launches a fireball at his unprotected chest, but the sizzle of fire doesn't slow him down. He summons an identical weapon out of thin air, and his reptilian nostrils flare. His lips move as though he's talking to her, but the murky fog muffles their conversation. Jules throws another fireball at him, but the snake-man holds his ground, his mouth stretched into a serpentine smile. With a snicker, he tastes the air with his bicuspid tongue.

Like Barron predicted, our magic is useless against them, and a hard ball forms in my throat.

Next to the small cockpit, Mallory sits in a lotus position, a series of demonic runes perfectly drawn on the white fiberglass in black chalk. Purple flames light her face.

Where the fuck is Barron?

Just as I'm about to write him off as dead, the Scot barrels into the fight from the other side of the bow, and the sight of him scatters chills up and down my neck.

Black tendrils stretch in a long, wispy cloak behind him—a shroud of night. The tattoos on his arms writhe along his forearms, forming black gloves, the solid ink running up to his elbows. Dark veins bury into his biceps like long, ethereal claws.

Two daggers absorb the light in his tar-licked hands, slender blades made of darkness that shine with a peculiar purple flare. My breath stutters at the sight. A pulse of ancient magic emanates from him and rattles the very fabric of my cells, as though his shadowy hands could reshape the world itself.

Barron slices heads and tails off, silent and quick in his attacks. The dark-purple blades act as extensions of his hands, his grip perfectly balanced and his precise movements deadly as can be.

Despite his obvious strength and skills, the odds aren't good. The endless throng of snakes doesn't relent, and for every one of them that dies or falls off the ship, two more waggle their tails up the sides of the boat. The thick fog prevents them from flinging their tridents from afar with accuracy, but even blind throws can hit flesh.

With feline grace, the Scot pirouettes through the air to avoid a zooming trident. The discarded weapon scrapes along the fiberglass, and I fly low to snatch it from the deck.

If magic won't kill these creatures, then I hope their own weapons will. I try to skewer the snake-man closest to Jules, but he takes advantage of my proximity to grab my ankle. Gold nails bury into my calf, but I blast us up into the air. When he draws blood, I soldier through and ram the tip of the trident through his arm.

He doesn't let go, and I pour all my magic out to fly higher. In his slitted pupils, I see fear. *Snakey* is afraid of heights.

Just when I'm about to run out of steam, he releases me and lands into the dark water below with a loud splash. I glance back to the ship as Barron slices through half a dozen monsters like a ninja.

Jules' chest is heaving.

We are clearly outnumbered, and yet, none of them dare to attack Mal. The demon sits in the center of her circle with her lids closed like a fucking yoga instructor, and the creatures skirt around her with wide eyes.

Jules stands right behind her—probably hoping the snakes won't hurl weapons at her while she's so close to the demon.

"Mal?" Barron shouts. "Now would be a good time to help!" A nasty cut runs from his pectoral to the space beneath his left arm, his shirt drenched with fresh blood.

Mallory squints harder, multiple lines creasing her forehead. "I can't transform."

"Ye better."

Mal tugs on her long curls and growls. "I can't. Jules, what are you waiting for? You're our only shot."

Jules spreads her arms wider. A perfect, tempestuous purple orb—its shade identical to Barron's blade—roars to life between her hands.

What in the Dark Mother's name is this shit?

Life keeps throwing me curveballs, and they are all shaped like my sister, who apparently draws infernal magic from the ether like a magician pulls rabbits out of a hat. The snake-men recoil—hell, even Barron pauses mid-fight to stare at her.

The purple orb stretches into four globulous, deadly spheres that bury inside the four closest snake men. Their bodies hit the ground a moment later, tongues spilling out of their mouths, eyes vacant.

Acid simmers at the back of my throat. First the healing, and now this? Is she even my sister? For the first time since I saved her life, I wonder if it's really her, or if the Jules I grew up with was somehow replaced by a shape-shifting creature strong enough to fool me, but I dismiss the thought immediately. One look at her, and my blood boils with pride—and jealousy. She's my Jules, whether she's still human or not. Did her marriage to Cole change the very fabric of her? That seems like a more reasonable explanation.

The shock caused by Jules' power ripples across the snake-men, and they slither to the edges of the boat. Guttural clicks and hisses reverberate across the fiberglass, but with a knowing look, they wiggle past the railings and slink back to the sea.

Barron yanks a limp body from the deck and dumps it into the water. "Well. Wouldn't ye know. We have a second demon aboard." His pointed glare lingers on Mallory, and I detect a hint of reproach.

Mallory lifts her chin up. "We all have our secrets. Jules' true nature wasn't mine to share."

I land near the cockpit, eyes fixed on Jules. Purple highlights already freckle her hair, and I observe her closely. "A demon? How are *you* a demon?"

She bites her bottom lip. "Dad lied to us about my mother."

"Your mother…"

"Was a demon, yes." Unshed tears glimmer in her blue eyes.

The tremble of power emanating from Barron wears off, and the black cloak and gloves dissolve into smoke. He staggers past us to the cabin.

I swallow hard, the lump in my throat thick and dry. "How long have you known?"

Jules grazes the demonic circle Mallory drew on the bridge with the tip of her shoe. "Not long. He told me over Christmas break."

I'm...baffled. Flabbergasted. Shocked. My jaw hangs open, and, while I expect to feel angry at being left out of the loop once again, I can't believe Dad lied to her for so long about something so... profound. I spent my entire life yearning for my mother's affection, but that Jules was denied the chance to even meet hers—

"Wait. How could he do this to you? Is she alive?"

Jules shakes her head. "He said she died right after I was born."

I wrap my arms around her and hold her tight. "I'm so sorry."

A hiccup quakes her chest. "Err—You're not worried about what it could mean for you? If people learned the truth..."

My sister is half-demon and married to a Fae prince...Clearly my political aspirations are doomed, but on this bizarro boat, in this savage realm filled with fog and monsters, I can't bring myself to care.

"I don't care."

A part of me simply...breaks. Despite mother's claims, I trust my sister. I love her. I'm never good enough for Piper anyway, never lady enough, never smart enough, never shrewd enough. Darkwood is a two-timing bitch, and Daniel lied to me for *months*.

I grip her hands tightly in mine. "You saved us, Jules. Demon or not, you saved us. And you looked so bad-ass doing it I could cry."

She wipes her teary eyes with her sleeve. "Thank you for saving me. Ever since I arrived at Dark Falls, we haven't been...friends. I'm not even sure why you were in the forest that night."

With a strangled sob, I pull her in for another hug. "You're right. We weren't friends, but we'll always be sisters. I would never let anyone hurt you, Jules. Never. Not Darkwood, or Daniel, or even my mom. Is that why you were able to heal yourself? Because you're a demon?"

"Not exactly, but I swear I'll explain everything in detail, and soon."

The fog from before lifts, probably created by Barron's or Mal's magic, and the underworld sun shines above our heads.

My chest warms. "I want us to be friends again."

We might not be ready to lay out all our secrets and compare notes, but it's a start. I'm not sure Jules can understand my ambitions. For her, standing out is...effortless.

Wherever she goes, Jules always ends up being the center of attention. Whether she's cast as the lead in the school play, or just becomes the glue that keeps friends together. She doesn't know what it feels like to wait patiently on the sidelines, unnoticed.

She rests her head on my shoulder. "Promise me, Allie. Promise me we won't end up on different sides of this fight again."

I rest my chin in her thick curls. "I promise."

We hug as sisters should, and for a moment, my heart isn't so raw anymore.

5

RED BARRON

Allie

*J*ules cranks up the lighting with a suspended fire orb and wipes her sweaty curls away from her face. "Stop moving, or I'll stick the needle in your eye," she growls at Barron.

The three of us huddle in the cabin while Mallory stands guard outside. The Scot sits on the blue bench by the kitchen table. Jules plans to stitch him up—with or without his consent.

I inventory the first aid kit and lay all useful gear beside the sink. A rag—drenched with blood—floats in a big bowl of hot water. We all had scrapes and bruises to tend to, but Barron not only has a three-pronged gash the size of my fist in his back, but he's also acting like a big baby about it.

The Scot mumbles profanities under his breath before he finally speaks up. "I don't need sutures—magical or otherwise. I need Scotch."

Jules' eye-roll echoes my exact sentiment toward the sailor as she passes me the needle. "Here. You do it. I'll find him some alcohol." She crouches and rummages through the cupboard below the sink.

The sight of the needle heats my neck, and I lick my lips. Blood isn't my forte. The last thing I want to do is sew up the huge slash in Barron's shoulder blade, but hey—here goes.

"Ow. Careful." He jerks away as I begin my displeasing chore.

"If you had healing cream, we wouldn't have to do this old school." We enchanted the needle and thread to glue the skin back together, but we couldn't do anything for the pain.

"I haven't crossed paths with a healer in years, and my magic isn't really made to put things back together," he grunts.

The ink covering his arms undulates beneath the skin, and I lean closer. The Celtic knots and Norse runes rearrange under my dumbfounded stare, like they're steering clear of the wound. "Your tattoos are moving."

Jules pauses her search to validate my observation. "Woah. That's freaky."

"Don't mind them. It's something they do."

"They're afraid to fall off or something?" Jules cracks.

Deep lines crease the corner of Barron's eyes. "Hurry up, the poison burns like hell."

The poison-coated weapon left some type of teal oil in his flesh. I wipe it off as best as I can with a fresh rag before taking a bite of the shredded muscle.

He snarls and cowers away.

"Stop moving, damn it." My brain searches for a distraction. "What were those things out there?" If he's busy *mansplaining*, he might settle down a bit.

"Nagas. They're close relatives to mermaids, but they worship the Old Gods. They used to be pretty peaceful—before the Scourge, that is."

Jules pours three shot glasses and passes one to each of us. "What happened to this realm? I think we earned the right to know."

Barron evaded most of our questions about himself, his powers, or the very realm we ended up in, like he wanted to protect its secrets as well as his own.

The Scot gulps the shot down in one swig and motions for Jules to pour him another. "Yer a demon, so I might as well tell ye. A hundred years ago, it used to be much like yer own. Cities bustled with merchants, horses, and sinners. Farmers and fishermen tended to their crops and nets in peace. Lesser demons were nothing more than fauna, while the most powerful ones ruled over the rest of the population.

"But the glory days of the Underworld are long gone. Hollows infested most of the continent and ravaged the castles, killing all but a few magic users. The demons that survived are the craftiest and deadliest of them all, and they rule over the islands with blood and violence. That is, until a hollow worms its way onto their lands, which is bound to happen at some point. A few non-magic creatures and humans have begun to rebuild the continent, but the likes of me and you wouldn't survive a day out there."

"So hollows can only infect magic users?" I clip off the thread and start a fresh stitch on the subcutaneous tissues. The muscles beneath already melded, so Jules' spell is working.

"Aye."

Jules screws back the cork of the Scotch bottle and lays it down next to the sink. "How did you summon those infernal blades?"

The shadowy power we witnessed out there isn't like anything we ever heard of growing up, and while Jules clearly keeps secrets of her own, it soothes me to know she's clueless on this, too.

"I told ye before. If ye want to know, you have to beat me at poker." The Scot's lips twitch in a half-smile, and he starts shuffling his cards.

With a huff, Jules hustles back to the bridge. Fire rumbles below the surface of her skin, her frustration palpable.

I smile at my—wildly impatient—patient and sink the needle deep in his flesh. "Stick that deck up your ass and tell me anyway. How do you summon infernal magic? Are you a demon?"

Like my sister...

He shoots me a sideways glance. "Nae."

"What are you doing in this realm, then?"

He slides a little deeper into the cushions. "I'm considered...undesirable by the current administration."

"Undesirable how?" I cut off the thread and start working on the skin.

He peers at me, eyes half-mast. "How old are you? Sixteen?"

My smile widens, and I keep a sugary, effable tone while tugging on the thread a little too hard. "I'm almost nineteen, you asshole."

"Ohh—big difference." He rolls his eyes. "Since yer a child, let me speak to you in terms ye'll understand. Yer government has become irrelevant and outdated. The Magisterium is a farce that lets monsters flourish in the four corners of the world. Darkwood is a plague that never ends. The whole system is corrupt, no matter who sits on the chair."

"Easy to say for a...Are you a smuggler, a thief, or what?"

He glimpses at my needle work. "Are you always so persistent?"

"I'm curious." I lean closer to his ear. Men react better to honey than venom, and I'm not naive. I've caught him stealing glances at me —this small boat isn't exactly private. Whatever he is, Barron is a warm-blooded man, and his relationship with Mallory is platonic.

Darkness hovers around him, an aura of raw energy rumbling over his skin—so potent I can almost touch it. Whatever magic he summoned before still runs thick in his veins.

"Curiosity killed the cat, little storm. Ye'll be happier if ye don't know," he whispers wryly.

"What are you hiding below deck?" I knot the last of the thread, the sutures done, and trace the line of his bicep up to his neck.

Goosebumps freckle his skin, but he jerks to his feet and spins around to face me. "The secrets I keep on *my* boat don't concern you."

We measure each other, the scissors still in my blood-stained hands. His chest heaves, and a few, long seconds pass before he yanks the bottle of Scotch from the counter and uncorks the top.

Mallory descends into the cabin, her glacial blue eyes clear and wide. "Come out now. We've got a problem."

Barron holds both his wounded arm and his bottle of Scotch close as we return outside.

"What the fuck?" I cry out.

A fat but terrifying white cyclone swirls over the dark Underworld sea in concentric circles. Clouds descend from it, forming a thick, opaque column that touches the surface of the water. Midnight-blue streaks wisp around it, glittering with magic, as though a thousand stars are playing hide and seek with my retinas. I check the mainsail, but the phenomenon doesn't wrinkle my crafted wind at all.

It's heading straight for us, and sweat gathers above my brows.

Jules clenches her fists. "I thought the portal was close by."

Barron holds the mainsail rope, ready to reel it in. "Aye. It's inside that cloud."

"It's a tempest. A big one," Mallory says on a sauntered breath, her face paler than it was before.

Barron swallows another swig of alcohol. "Time in the underworld is tricky. When two wildly antagonistic time zones collide, it creates a ripple in the continuum. A temporal fold, if you will."

"Is it dangerous?" I ask.

"It'll make for an interesting voyage, that's for sure." Discarding his bottle, he grabs the rudder with both hands, ready to steer us into the grim anomaly. "Ye ready?"

Him and his damned tapped *R's*. I give him a curt nod.

He motions to the railing. "Ye better hold on tight, lass. This storm isn't the kind you can control." Without breaking a sweat he steers us directly inside the clouds.

A wave of magic crashes through me, and I feel as though we're not quite being roughed up by the tall waves, but rather being *sucked* into a dark hole. The agitated sea forms tall walls of black, murky water around the boat, their length quickly stretching above the mainsail. All my wind vanishes in the anomaly, like it cannot coexist with even the slightest breeze.

I hold my breath. Deep vibrations resonate in my bones. Boom. Boom. *Boom.* I feel as though a monster just squeezed me in its claws before dipping me into a thick, spicy tub of jelly. Shaking out my hands to get rid of the painful tingles, I force a tiny breath down my lungs.

When we emerge on the other side, the oily shade of the Underworld sea vanishes, and the clouds above our heads melt from purple to gray. Fog licks the cliffs in the distance, and the salty sting of the ocean tickles my nose.

Ice bites into my cheeks and arms, and deep shivers tremble down my spine, but other than that, I'm okay.

Barron swipes a hand above his brow. "Phew."

A heart-wrenching mewl scratches the air. Mallory is gone, replaced by the dark furred jaguar. I avert my gaze, my mortal instinct already screaming at me to run at the mere sight of the cursed demon.

We made it back to Earth, but the open ocean stretches as far as the eye can see.

I click my tongue. "We're nowhere near Dark Falls."

"Calm down, princess."

I point to Jules. "She's the princess, not me." There's no way he can't tell us apart, so the sly, filthy sailor just wants to rub my nose in it.

"Then how come yer the one acting lek one?"

He doesn't mean it as a compliment, and I whip my head around so I don't flip him off. I won't give in to his bad manners. I'll rise above.

Jules fails to stifle a giggle with her palm, and a snort escapes her as she waltzes under the boom and joins Barron by the mainsail.

I head down the length of the boat, staring out at the sea.

Onyx prances over to me, her mouth half-open, and her eyes crinkled at the edges.

"You're laughing at me, too, huh?"

The knee-jerk reaction to flee that first hit me at the sight of the feline recedes, and I realize its presence no longer affects me the way it did before I traveled to the Underworld. Is it because I know it's Mallory, or because my trip to the most secret and damned realm has left its mark? I'm not sure.

The wind blows my hair forward as I watch the soft waves. We might have survived the Nagas' attack and the tempest, but we're far from safe. A tiny part of me wishes I could disappear inside the blue expanse of the ocean and never return to Dark Falls. So much pain awaits me there...

Jules joins me by the railing. "Barron says we'll get to Dark Falls before sunrise."

I tighten the jacket around my frame. "We've got a lot of work to do."

She leans on the banister, her hands linked, and glances at me sideways. "So...you will keep my secret?"

A sigh escapes me. "You're my sister, Jules. That won't ever change." I tried to distance myself from her to please Piper, but in doing so, I almost lost her. No more.

Her dark curls fly in the breeze as she offers me her hand. "So...Together?"

I grip her fingers and squeeze. "Together."

6

KANSAS

Jules

"Here we are, lass. The promised land." With Allie's wind at our backs, Barron steers his ship into Dark Falls' bay.

A bright moon shines above our heads. The familiar shape of the cliffs twists my heart, and I instinctively reach for the phantom stab wound in my side.

The mainsail flaps as my sister nuances her magic.

Barron anchors his boat. "The water's too shallow. I can't go any further. We'll have to tender out."

Allie huffs. "I can fly."

Rolling his eyes, the Scot lowers the sleek fiberglass canoe that was strapped to the railings into the water. Small waves splash the hull as I climb down inside the canoe and grab one of the paddles at the bottom. Barron motions for me to sit at the front and takes the seat at the back.

We glide along the bay, and the distance between us and the beach quickly melts.

The blade of my paddle waddles in the water like an ugly duckling learning to swim, probably doing more harm than good. A pirate's life? Not for me.

The sun winks over the horizon, revealing flecks of orange and yellow in the trees, and I groan. "We missed the whole summer? Fuuck. You'll be late to your thing in Miami."

"Don't worry about it." Barron's muscles flex as he rows with ease and skill.

The front of the boat glides along the beach with a soft *swish,* and I jump to my feet, about ready to kneel down and kiss the sand.

Allie lands next to me.

"Thanks again. For everything," I tell Barron. We already established he has no interest in crossing paths with anyone from our world.

Barron uses the pummel of his oar to push the boat away from shore. "I'll wait for an hour in the bay...In case you don't like what ye find."

My sister wraps her arms around her chest. "Why wouldn't we like what we find?"

With a quiet, lopsided grin, the Scot rolls his shoulders and starts rowing back to *Lettie.*

"You ready?" I ask Allie.

"No." She digs her heels into the sand. "Dark Falls was broken, Jules. Celeste Draco watered down the curriculum so supernaturals wouldn't study the most advanced spells. She schemed to boot mortals out and deliberately undermined the other professors to better control us. Whatever happens, we can't allow her to be in charge again."

I gaze at the cliffs and imagine what Allie sees in them. "I have no issue with that analysis. Celeste is an A-class bitch."

Her eyes widen, her blue gaze vulnerable and open. "Really? You married her son and you won't defend her?"

"I'm not saying Fae are *perfect*. I love Cole, but he's not always *right*. In fact, the dynamics of his court are pretty fucked up. But Fae aren't inherently bad as Dad taught us. We would all grow stronger by opening our minds a little."

Tears fill Allie's eyes. "Beth didn't deserve to die. There's so much guilt weighing on me, Jules. So many regrets. If only I'd compared notes with you, if only I hadn't trusted Daniel so blindly..."

"Shh. Come here." I wrap her up in my arms.

"All my life, I just wanted Piper to *like* me. I know she's been nothing but horrible to you, but she's my mother. I just got her back, Jules. If she dies..." A hiccup pops out of her mouth.

"If I still had the horn, and Beth's soul was at rest, I would give it back."

I will never forgive Piper for how she treated me, but I really hope we can find another way to cure her disease. *For Allie's sake.*

"What happened? Did the Fae take it from you?" she asks.

My gaze flies to the sand. "Cole used it...on me."

"*On* you?" Her brows pull together. "Is that how you healed?"

"Yes."

She licks her lips. "He used it on you...to make you immortal?"

I give her a small nod and watch her face for a tell, but she appears to be stunned, not resentful.

"Wow. That's...he must really love you."

I grimace at the obvious surprise, but Allie walks away.

I know my sister, and if she's ready to change the subject, I won't torture us both further by discussing my unexpected immortality. If the roles were reversed, I'd be jealous as hell.

The stairs Cole and I destroyed that fateful day on the beach when he fled the realm with Brie have been rebuilt with steel railings and freshly-painted wood, so our ascension is quick and painless.

The dining hall's windows are obscured. A forcefield shimmers behind the building, and I run over to it. The semi-translucent wall emits a powerful energy signature. A tree snuggles up to the force-field, close enough for me to recognize its blurry form, but everything else beyond it blurs into a white void. I graze the barrier with my fingertips only to be blasted back several feet.

Ow.

Gravel bites into my ass as I rub my head.

Allie clicks her tongue. "Careful."

I dust off my pants and stand. "Something's not right. Can you feel it?"

"The vibrations of power? Yep." She brings a hand to her chest. "It's like standing in the middle of a rock and roll concert."

"It's...wild."

The unsteady thuds spark off in a series of uneven beats. Energy drums through the land below us, and I walk around the corner of the building to look through the large floor-to-ceiling windows.

Allie catches up to my rear. "Is the force field meant to keep hollows in or out?"

The dining hall's tables lay on their sides, many of them in shambles. Arrows and swords stick out of the furniture.

"What do you think happened here?" Allie asks.

I boost myself through the broken window and graze the closest blade. "Nothing good. Hollows don't use swords, right?" The itch at the back of my skull spreads to my spine. We missed more than the summer; we missed a battle of some kind. The weapons are without a doubt Fae-made. Threads of copper and silver adorn the hilts, like the ones the soldiers held at the palace, and my breath stutters. What did Cole do when I didn't return?

A high, frighteningly familiar hiss curdles my blood.

White smoke whistles out from the debris, only a few paces in front of me.

"Jules, get out!" Allie shouts at my back.

"Fuck." I spin around and leap through the broken window.

A piece of glass digs deep into my leg, but I pry it off with a wince, not stopping for a second as we run back toward the cliffs. Did Barron know hollows waited for us here? Did he sense them, somehow?

Allie slows down. "They're not chasing after us. They seem corralled inside the walls."

I spin around and realize she's right. "The one good thing so far."

The white veil hisses at our backs. Beams of sunrise reflect off the hollows' wispy tails, but they don't venture out of the building.

Allie grips my arm and observes me from all angles. "One of them touched you."

I pat down my chest and sides, checking for bite marks—or a sign of infection. "I'm okay."

"Are you sure? I saw a shape on your forehead." She tucks my curls behind my ears, eyes glued to the space above my brows.

"Is it still there? What did it look like?"

"A…star, I think. It's gone now." She presses her lips together. "The horn. Did it give you some type of power against hollows?"

What a nice thought, but I shake my head. "Not that I'm aware of."

If it did, I'm not inclined to test that theory until I'm *absolutely* sure of the outcome.

She stares down the magic wall with both hands on her hips. "Listen. The force field must not run very far up. I could probably fly beyond it. It's super strong, so someone must be tending to it on the other side. I'll have them build a door for you."

Unless it's Oz, or Darkwood, or whatever Fae soldiers came through here…"We don't have many other options."

"I'll be quick. If I'm not back in fifteen minutes to let you know what's up, or if the hollows stick their nasty snouts out of the building, run back to Barron and wait on the boat for me to return. It'll be less creepy than here."

I nod. "Alright."

We find a clear space along the force field, away from the unending forest and the dining hall. The flat landscape offers a wide view of our surroundings, and it's close to the path leading back to the beach. I'm confident I could outrun the hollows if needed. They're scary as hell, but slow.

Allie's lips quirk. "Don't be all Jules and go risking your life for nothing. I'm on it, okay?"

"Okay." I sit on a nearby rock to wait.

She blasts off into a vertical flight. I follow her shrinking silhouette until she dips over the edge of the force field.

Seagulls flap their wings above my head, and their high-pitched quacks irk my nerves. Icy shivers rock my spine as I check on the hollows again, but the white fog no longer hangs in the air, as though the creatures have gone back to sleep.

I rub my forehead, trying to recall if one of them really touched me. An itch above my hip tickles, and I raise the hem of my shirt to scrape the skin. I do recall a sharp pinch in my side as I ran, around the same time as the piece of glass dug inside my leg, but it could have been a muscle cramp. Only...a star is too precise to be a figment of Allie's imagination. Did Beth's *gifts* include a special ability to repel these monsters? Or was the apparition on my forehead merely a warning that a hollow was about to claim my soul?

Just as I'm about to relax, the arrhythmic current of magic drums a staccato in my veins, and I jolt to my feet.

A few paces to my right, a vertical tear stretches to life with dazzling blue hues, different enough not to look like another Underworld portal, but similar enough to steal my breath. Is the whole realm now torn at the seams? How can that be?

Two Fae slip out of the fresh portal. Black and silver uniforms are visible under their yellow-tinted armor, and my stomach almost leaps out of my throat. Their gaze latches on to me, and to be frank, I'm thrilled to see them.

"Is that a Faerie portal?" I ask.

The men stiffen and raise their swords. While their garbs are identical, one of them appears to be decades younger than his partner.

"Your presence here is forbidden. By the powers of the Seelie King, I'm placing—" The rehearsed speech dies on the young soldier's lips, and he elbows his colleague's side. "By Queen Mab, she's exactly like the last one. What do we do?"

"What can we do? We take her to the King," the older one replies.

"He'll be in a mood..."

Apparently, I breached a Fae war zone or something. They dash closer in unison, their lethal weapons directed at me.

With a mild infernal burst, I flatten the young one to the ground. "This is a misunderstanding. Please let me explain."

I pirouette away from the more experienced soldier and build a tiny infernal orb in my palm to disarm him. I don't want to kill them since they're working for Cole's father, but I need them to drop their swords to the ground and put their listening ears on.

Before I can explain the gist of my predicament, a forceful blow at the back of my neck sends me flying head-first into the mud. Cold metal ensnares my wrists, and the lull of a magic-bind snuffs out my powers.

A thick brown splat of mud sticks to my forehead as I crane my neck around to see my attacker.

A third soldier with a full-sized chainmail glares down at me. Recognition registers on his face even though I'm convinced I've never seen him before. "Always shackle them first, Jayden."

"Sorry, boss."

I struggle in my restraints. "Let me go. I'm a Fae princess." I've never played the princess card before, but it's a good time to start. If he recognized me, why the hell would he lead with the cuffs?

A white strip of fabric prevents me from speaking further. The *boss* tightens the gag viciously over my mouth and glowers with a spark of hatred so intense, you'd think I murdered his entire family.

One of the other two flings a bag over my head. "The King will have our heads."

I can't see a thing, and my pulse fanfares in my ears.

Two pairs of hands haul me forward, but I wrestle to break free. Mute and blind and without magic, I've still got my muscles. The men clearly didn't expect me to try my luck in a physical fight and release me.

Only, instead of freedom, I fall square on my face. Muddy water seeps through the fabric covering my head. I spit out a curse against the gag and crawl to my feet, but the soldiers grasp my arms once more, this time with more strength and ire.

"Stogg…We should throw her over the cliff and be done with her," one soldier mumbles. "No one has to know."

A hand presses hard on my forehead, and soft, ancient Fae lyrics graze my ear, whispered by their leader. The hushed chant squeezes my stomach before my heartbeats grow sluggish, and everything melts into darkness.

7

SENTINELS

Allie

The tall pines of the unending forest pepper the yellow, red, and orange leaves with dark green freckles, the beauty of autumn on full display. Beyond the forcefield, Dark Falls looks as normal as can be, though the solid magical wall stretches over half a mile. A golden sunrise frames the Dark Falls library. The building clashes with the worn-down dining hall on the other side, its windows in perfect condition. The glow of the library's world-renowned chandelier acts as a beacon of hope, and I breathe a little easier as I land on the gravel path.

The hollows might have attacked Dark Falls, but they didn't win.

My mouth dries up...if Dark Falls stands, then Daniel might still be headmaster. Maybe he's even in the library, or in his cabin.

I rub my sweaty palms down my pants. I promised myself to dump him, but now that I'm actually here...Doubts swarm my heart.

Before I find the courage to take another step, a familiar figure stops dead in its tracks on the other side of the floor-to-ceiling glass panes.

Lydia Hawks gapes from the inside of the building. Her arms fall to her sides, and the book in her hands tumbles to the ground.

The evident surprise in the curve of her brows and her awe-struck demeanor spark an itch between my shoulder blades. I crane my neck around to check if something else in the vicinity might explain her reaction, but she jolts into action and rushes to the door.

"Allie?" she shouts from the top of the staircase.

The stone gargoyles glower at the outburst and turn their backs to her.

"Hey, Lydia." Last time we talked, she made it clear how much she hated me, so I can't explain the joy on her face.

A long red braid falls over her shoulder, longer than it should be, and I start to wonder if more than a few months have gone by.

She descends the steps two at a time. "It's really you." She clasps my arms. "Is Jules with you? Is she alive?"

Oh, I guess we've been missing for a while. "She's behind the force-field. We need to let her in."

"Jules is alive. I knew it." She doubles back up the library stairs and wrenches open the door. "Rose! Come, quickly." The chandelier flickers at the sudden burst of wind.

The gargoyles flap their wings at my approach, their stony heads tilted to the side.

Rose Deveraux, the infamous Spells and Sorcery teacher, appears at the top of the stairs. The stylish pencil skirt and blazer she usually wears to class have been replaced by jeans and a white, v-neck t-shirt that emphasizes her black skin. The casual ensemble throws me for a loop. Beautiful braids flatten her hair to her scalp, giving her a young, hip look, but her intense gaze settles on me, ever so intimidating. "Allison Winslow?"

Lydia paces in front of the main entrance. "It's really her."

"Which means..." Deveraux whispers.

Lydia's green eyes shine with tears, the cracks in her voice filled with unbridled joy. "Yes. Jules is alive."

Deveraux presses her hand to her heart, as though my sister being alive solves all her problems and then some. After a heavy, sauntered breath, she hurries down the stairs. Her black boots crunch in the gravel as she grips my arm. "Where is she?"

"Wait a minute. What's going on?"

Lydia runs past us, the flaps of her checkered jacket wafting in the wind. "There'll be time for questions later. Let's get Jules first." She raises a hand to the force field and cuts a doorway in the impregnable wall.

I run to the other side. "Jules?"

"Julia?" Deveraux yells over the wind.

"Where the fuck did she go?" I mumble under my breath, certain the fifteen minutes we agreed on haven't passed, yet.

The cliffs offer a wide view of the bay—and Barron's boat. The beach is empty, and there is no way Jules could have rowed back to the ship in so little time. I scan the dining hall, but no hollow lurks along the confines of the building.

Lydia grips my shoulder. "She's gone. The Fae patrol must have gotten to her first. How did you get here?"

"We used a boat to sail back." I point to Lettie, waddling in the bay.

Deveraux squints at the sea. "You found a sailing boat in the Underworld?"

"Something like that. Why is a Fae patrol gallivanting around the academy?" I dig my heels in the grass. Nothing makes sense. "What the fuck happened to Dark Falls? I need to know *everything*."

8

ALL TIED UP

Jules

Cold water splashes my chest, and I jolt awake, the bag still propped over my head.

"Wake up, coconut," a man says in a typical sprite accent.

Hands tied above my head, I stand on my tiptoes, struggling to bear my weight. The magic shackles have metallic spikes that dig deep into my wrists, and my muscles scream in agony at the prolonged stretch.

"I'll remove the bag. Stay calm," a quiet voice grumbles.

I squint at the light. A sprite and the Fae soldier that shackled me earlier stand stock-still in front of me.

"Fuck," the sprite whines.

The soldier rubs the arch of his brow. "I told you so."

I dangle from a beam holding a medium-sized war tent up. A slit in the fabric acts as a door on the opposite side of the tent. Not one sound pierces the red tarps, and the slit is perfectly sealed, so I suspect a privacy spell shields us from the outside world.

Pointy strands of grass prickle the soles of my bare feet. A water glass sits on a mahogany table in the back of the tent, along with an array of weapons, and the sight sparks an itch on my tongue. It's been a weird day, and I wouldn't mind gulping down cold water, but I'm still gagged.

The sprite's parched wings twitch at his back. "The King will be here in a minute."

"I'm off, then. Good luck." The soldier slips through the tent's exit and disappears from view.

With a wet rag, the sprite washes off my forehead and nose, but not in a gentle, helpful way. No, the fiend rubs my face like he wants to erase it, and I take advantage of his closeness to head-butt him.

He hisses and snaps my necklace off my neck. "Where did you find that?" His face crumples, and he turns the emerald pendant in his gnarly hands like it means something to him before he wraps it up in a rag.

I'm gagged, so it's not as though I can answer him.

The Fae King waltzes into the tent with no drums or trumpets, and the two red flaps seal themselves behind him. I've seen him before, though not in the way I was expecting.

Air blows out of my lungs, and my eyes widen.

"By the Dark Gods and their wicked brooms," I curse despite the gag, but the sounds that come out are unintelligible.

He's the King of Faerie. What the fuck happened while I was gone?

Does this make me *queen*?

Holy shit!

Raw power rushes off Cole in spicy, drugging waves. His dark ringlets have been cut short, and the look gives him a severe edge. The shape of his shoulders is the same—yet different.

Metal scrapes against wood in a loud *screech* as I tug on the chains. All the hairs at the back of my neck stand erect, and a molten heat radiates through my body.

My bound powers melt me from the inside out.

A network of blueish, silvery scars gleams on his neck. The patterns are mesmerizing, but they tug and twist at my heart.

Unseelie claws leave a permanent mark. Always.

Each one of them highlights a wound he didn't have the last time I saw him. Every violent line is a crack that separates us, like wrinkles marking the passage of time.

Oh no, no, no...the cyclone, or tempest as Mal called it...Allie and I thought we'd missed the summer, but we clearly missed *more*.

Cole squints at me as though I'm a puzzle that needs solving. Under his scrutiny, I'm nothing but a goblin's flea that he longs to crush under his foot, and while I remember our last fight vividly, I do not think I deserve this much ire.

My surprise and elation to be reunited with Cole—the Fae King!—condenses into an unbearable pressure in my belly.

What happened to him? How long was I gone?

The sprite rubs the sharp angle of his nose. "I could deal with it myself, Sire."

"Leave me, Jameson," Cole says, the growl so dark and deep, I hardly recognize his voice.

"As you wish." Jameson flaps his wings and whistles out with a sullen pout, taking my damn necklace in his grubby paws.

Cole snaps off his armor plate, the black Faerie clothes underneath embroidered with copper, brass, and silver accents, and grabs a dagger from the desk.

My eyes bulge, but all I can do is wiggle in my restraints. My stiff muscles scream from the effort.

He rips the belt off my body, working quietly to undress me. At first, I assume it's sexual, but the hard clench of his jaw and the bunch of his muscles quicken my breath. He pats down my waist and under-arms, and I realize he's merely searching me.

No kinky reunion sex in the schedule, and it hits me. He doesn't believe that I'm *me*. He's questioning a *prisoner*.

When he's satisfied that I've got no weapons or spells hidden on my person, he turns his attention to the gag. The rough calluses of his hands scratch my cheek, and his amber eyes look everywhere but in mine. "You're not the first one they've sent. It's useless to try and fool me."

He scrapes away a layer of mud from my temple with the blade. "You're not even a good copy. You're a filthy, scrawny thing."

Excuse me?

I pull my feet off the ground to kick his shin, but fail.

The edge of the blade sinks inside my belly button. "I want you to think long and hard about the answers you will give me, because the wrong ones will compel me to gut you."

I swallow hard and nod. He's not kidding. If he's certain that I'm an impostor, how can I convince him otherwise—and quickly?

We're like Romeo and Juliet, except Romeo will skewer Juliet before she can let him know she's not really dead. How about that for a violent ending?

A bitter pout twists his face as he grazes my tricolored curls, the purple and red strands somehow angering him further. "My soldiers swear they saw you use infernal magic. How did you conjure it?" He slices off the gag with his dagger.

The sting in my cheek tells me it left a bloody line.

"I have it inside me," I croak, testing my voice.

Sharp interest registers on his features. "You're a demon? What kind?"

"The kind you used to like."

The obscurion nudges the tender skin of my throat.

Okay. Flirting won't work. What else?

Think, Jules!

What else?

"Last chance, demon. Truth or death."

"Let's make a deal. I'll talk, but you have to vow to let me go afterwards. Otherwise, you'll gut me regardless." The Cole I know is always itching to strike a deal, especially with his enemy.

"Torture will get me the same results. Let's find out what amount of pain is enough for you to drop your glamor."

A low pinch stings my neck, and blood drips to the space between my breasts as Cole carves into me. I look up to the chains tied around my wrists and concentrate on the pressure of their hold not to scream.

"If you kiss me now, your debt will be paid in full," I chant in prayer, hoping my husband has got better memory than instinct.

He said those exact words to me before we had sex for the first time.

The blade stops.

Cole whips back with such force that he stumbles backward. "What did you say?" The low growl reverberates off the tent walls.

I convey all the weight of the last few months—years for him, clearly—into a bone-chilling gaze. "You heard me."

"How do you know that?"

My chest expands. "Make a deal with me, and I'll tell you who I really am."

He tugs hard on my hair. "By the Dark Gods, I won't harm you if you tell me the whole truth about who you are and who sent you here."

"I swear it," I vow.

Magic pulses in the air.

A long exhale whizzes out of my chest. "I'm Jules, Cole. Allie flew us through the underworld portal seconds after Darkwood fucking shanked me, and I've been trying to get back to Dark Falls—to you—for *weeks*. I have no idea how much time passed here, but I'm stupidly confused—*and* thirsty." I wince at the soreness in my arms, suddenly lightheaded.

This is not happening. I'm dreaming. I must be, I mean—

"Oh, and Onyx tagged along. She's a woman, did you know that? A bit intense, but a woman." I'm breathless and half-mad. "You're the King of Faerie. Dark Falls was nuked by the hollows. Gods know if Dad is still alive, or Lydia. How can underworld time zones be so fucked up?" I swallow hard, eyes glued to the scars on Cole's neck. "Please tell me I bumped my head and this is not real."

A coarse breath flutters down the valley between my breasts. "Tell me your name."

"Jules."

Cole squeezes my cheeks hard with one hand, and his amber gaze slithers inside me like it wants to hook my brains out. "Your whole name."

I attempt to kick his shin again, and this time, the feeble blow hits. "I'm Jules Winslow, your Gods-damn bride."

Cole holds me to him, one hand braced behind my neck. I struggle in his grip, my arms still tied above my head. The chains whine at the stretch, and my muscles scream in pain.

"Cole, I'm going to faint. Can you untie me?"

He doesn't respond, so stoic and immobile in the embrace that I'm not so much being *hugged* by my husband as I'm being *crushed* by a shredded, defined, and perfectly rock-solid statue of the Fae King.

I'm not sure he heard me at all. "Untie me, maybe? Cole?"

He snaps out of whatever hell his mind was buried in and doubles back toward the tent's slitted entrance. His arm shoots out, and he half-chokes an underling to death as he pulls him inside the tent. "Dig Trent Darkwood out of the oubliettes and bring him to me."

9

FRACTURED KING

Jules

"Untie me," I plead. The throb in my arms blurs my vision.

My bound powers still burn my insides, and I'm both hot and cold, suffocating under the thrall of the Fae King—and his stubbornness. An aftertaste of blood and sweat sticks to the air. The light boxes illuminating the tent flicker to an unnatural wind.

"I need a minute." Cole steals a glance at me and immediately looks away like I'm the sun and he forgot his fucking sunglasses.

"My arms hurt." I realign myself with the beam, my muscles shaking from the struggle. My toes scramble to find footing, and darkness creeps at the edge of my vision.

He stares at the ceiling. "You're dead."

"I'm obviously not."

The Fae King smudges his thumb in the half-dried blood on my cheek and gazes down at it in wonder.

"What the fuck is an oubliette?" I choke, ready to succumb to the shadows.

"A cold, forgotten dungeon." Cole's voice melts into a breathless, intimate drawl. With a trembling hand, he traces the deeper wound he carved on my neck. By the itch, I figure it's almost completely healed.

I lick my lips. "Why is Trent in a dungeon?"

He slides one hand around my throat, his palm hot and rough. The touch packs an ambivalent punch, and I can see he's still torn between crushing me *to him* or straight-up crushing *me*. "Because you're dead."

My gaze flicks to his lips. "I'm obviously not," I repeat quietly. "I will pass out, though."

He holds up my weight, his free arm braced below my ass, and relief washes through me. Fae magic presses around us, its pulse palpable inside the tent. The pain wanes to a dull, languid ache, and my body throbs under the King's call. I long to kneel in front of him more than I need to breathe.

His lids flutter. "Your voice..." He drags his nose along the slope of my neck. "Your scent." His tongue darts out to sample the trickle of blood. "Your taste..."

"It's me."

"It can't be." He keeps his eyes screwed shut like he's afraid to look again and find a flaw in this *copy* of me and plants a bittersweet kiss on my ear.

My stomach flip-flops, my heart drowned by a wave of hurt and anguish. Cole simply looks...fractured. Hollow. Desperate.

"Look at me," I whisper.

He shakes his head in denial.

A loud exhale rocks my lungs. "I'm still pissed that you made me immortal without my consent. But I missed you, more."

One hand tangled in my curls, Cole crushes his mouth to mine.

The kiss is savage and vicious. The bitter, earthy taste of mud fills my senses.

For me, it's meant to erase the time spent apart, the forsaken weeks down under that should have had no consequence, but that will clearly re-write our future. For every fresh scar I can see, a thousand more lurk beneath.

For him, I think it's still an indulgence. A moment of pretend, like he's happy to lose his mind in the impossibility of my existence and run with it for a few delirious laps.

Without looking, he tears the chains straight off the beam, his biceps straining at the effort. Chunks of wood fall along with them, and I both marvel and cower at the new ridges in his arm, the new shape of his chest. I link my arms around his neck, and the metal links cascade down his back. Skin, tongues, and lips fight for friction.

Until I pull away.

"How long was I gone?" A question that scares me more than this shredded, anachronistic Cole.

He doesn't answer. In the tick of his jaw and the terrible squint of his eyes, I can tell the answer will ruin me. A couple of years, maybe? Gods, let it not be more than three...

He packs me over his shoulder, holding the back of my knees. Another round of fire melts my insides as I abandon myself to his grasp, content that the slice-me-darling section of our reunion is over.

Despite the shock, thirst, and mind-boggling revelations, a thrill tickles through me. The spicy scent of leather and peaches soothes my raw nerves. I'm home.

A grassy path wide enough to count as a road awaits us outside. Across from the interrogation tent, an immense black and gold marquee bristles in the wind. Two soldiers stiffen at our approach, but Cole barrels past them.

Contrary to the one they chained me in, Cole's tent is cozy and warm. Magic lights flicker in heavy-duty metal cubes, the light boxes stacked on top of one another in the corners. The war room holds a large table, weapons, and a few comfortable seats, the grass covered with a thick carpet.

Fae do war in style.

Jameson spins around to face us. "You were quite quick—"

Cole raises his index finger. "Not a word." He navigates through the many rooms of the marquee. Past the war room, I catch glimpses of a dining room, a kitchen, a bedroom...

Identical square boxes light the Fae King's bed, the black covers perfectly tucked over the double-sized mattress. Crates pepper the corner, each of them easy to pick up and move should the need arise.

"You downgraded your bed," I tease.

Cole acknowledges my attempt at light conversation with a grunt.

My heart pulses, a sore wound in my chest, but I can't help but try to lighten the mood. Everything changed while I was gone, and I'm sure being Fae queen will be the least of my worries. The details of the royal war tent are an excuse not to ask more questions, a reprieve from all the answers that could destroy me.

Cole doesn't spread me on his bed as I'd hoped. Instead, he hauls me to the back of the bedroom, the space occupied by a free-standing tub. Fluffy, white towels hang from a rack nearby.

Cole deposits me to my feet, grabs a small flask on the vanity, and drops it inside the golden tub. Instantly, it fills to the brim.

Bubbles glisten in the warm light of the tent.

I blink a few times. "You want me to take a bath? Now?"

"Yes."

Sometimes, life just throws you a bubble bath.

A large oval-shaped mirror behind the tub reflects the absurdity of the situation as Cole breaks the link between the metal shackles and pulls the chains off, leaving the metal bracelets on.

He crosses his arms over his chest, his feet firmly planted in the plush carpet at our feet.

Heat licks my ribs. "You want me to bathe *in front of you*?"

"I need to examine you without all that mud, and I'm not letting a *prisoner* out of my sight."

"Cole. I mean—I'm all for some personal hygiene, but—"

He slithers forward. "Do it."

"Alright. Alright."

I peel off the muddy clothes, the pants and underwear first, my shirt long enough to cover my ass. I fumble with the thin camisole. Dust and grime have fused the fabric to my skin.

Cole's amber gaze prickles wherever it travels.

Fire swells in my chest, the lines visible under my skin.

I pull the top over my head, and Cole draws in a sharp intake of breath. My reflection in the mirror justifies his claim that I'm a filthy, scrawny thing. I've lost weight on the boat, but I made it through the Underworld sea. Each of my visible rib should celebrate that victory.

My flames swirl, unable to pierce the binding spell.

I snap off the bra and cower inside the bubbles, the thick foam shielding me from Cole's gaze. The hot water feels...sublime. I haven't had more than a toilet-shower combo in weeks.

My mind reels as it considers how many showers and baths Cole has had in my absence. He doesn't look at all inclined to join me, stiff as he is with a dark expression on his face. The kiss we shared earlier appears to be long forgotten.

I grab the soap on the ledge of the tub and start rubbing myself down, making a show of it. When I wash my breasts, I catch him wiggle slightly in the mirror. A grin tugs at the corners of my mouth.

I close my eyes and immerse myself completely.

After our fight, I tried to stay mad at him. I was furious that Dark-wood double-crossed me and justified Cole's actions. I'm still unnerved at how effortlessly he played me into drinking the damn potion, but as I am now, naked in front of the Fae King...I can't help but wish we could put it all behind us.

I'll stow my anger inside one of these war crates and unpack it later.

Right now, I want to seduce my estranged husband into my bath and kiss him until the distance between us thins and pops like one of the bubbles stuck to my skin.

Cole grips the underside of the vanity, his arms close to his body, his hands tucked underneath his elbows like he's holding himself off from reaching for me. I switch sides to meet his stare.

A low rumble passes his lips.

Water glides along my arms, and my dark curls stick to my back and neck. My chest heaves at the captive fire in my body.

I stick one leg out of the bath and scrub it down, then the other.

The bar of soap slowly travels past the kink of my knee to my thigh and plunges past the surface of the water to the space between my legs.

Cole's nostrils flare. He inches forward, and his gaze slips down the curve of my neck to my breasts. He schools it back up with a flash of teeth. "Stop it."

I hold an arm out. "Come here."

"Enough games. Dry yourself off."

My forehead creases. "Games?"

The hard clench of his jaw allows one, rushed breath. "It's been eleven years and four months since you stepped through that mirror."

My arm falls inside the tub with a loud *plop*.

All the confidence and bravado drains out of me in one cold, tight inhale. Fuck.

Eleven years...

I can't—

"Eleven years?" I squeak. I expected two—maybe four. Five was my worst-case scenario, and only because of Cole's scars.

Water splashes to the carpet as I abruptly stand up, snatch a towel from the rack, and wrap it around my frame. "Where is my dad? Is he alright? What happened to Oz and Darkwood? Did you check on Lydia? What about Flynn, where is he?" I search the room like I expect the blond Fae to materialize at the mention of his name. Questions and fears mingle on my breath, my brain going ten miles a minute, the implications of the news jumbling into chaos.

I consider my grumpy husband in a new light. Did Cole meet someone else? Is there another Fae queen?

"Sire?" Jameson calls from afar. "The vampire is here."

"Let him in," Cole's eyes never leave me, the weight of them sparking unhealthy tremors in my flesh.

Even with his long brown hair slicked back behind his ears and his soldier's uniform, Trent Darkwood doesn't look so different. He enters the room with a makeshift blindfold tied around his head.

"Took you long enough," Cole says to the vampire.

Trent offers him a fake smile, his arms held out in front of him.

"You posted me in this hole. Was the damn blindfold really necessary?"

"Yes," Cole croaks.

Posted? My brows furrow. I see no future where Trent now *works* for Cole.

"Are you taking a bath or something? The scent of jasmine and honey is so thick, I can't smell anything else."

What fucked-up alternate universe did I end up in?

Trent squares his shoulders. "Should I be worried? If you want me to serve your sexual needs, I'd like to be told upfront."

"Stop fucking around." Cole walks over to me, his gaze so dangerous that I hold the towel closer to my chest. "There's no magic in the three realms that can fool a vampire's taste for blood—especially blood he's tasted before. Be quiet and hold out your hand."

He wants to verify my identity *again*? How paranoid has he become?

I tuck the corner of the towel more securely under my armpit.

"Here. Taste her," Cole breathes.

Trent swallows hard, all the dark humor from before wiped from his features. "You want me to *bite* your guest?"

"*Delicately.*"

"Alright."

With a begrudging nose wrinkle, I offer Trent my arm. The vampire spins my wrist around and brings it to his lips.

How ironic is it that Cole is now asking Trent to bite me, when he was so enraged by our relationship? I must be dreaming. If anything, the vampire looks better than the last time I saw him. His chainmail fails to mask the thickness of his biceps, and despite the craziness of the situation, he seems more...at peace.

Long white fangs pierce my skin, and I blink to hide a wince.

Trent's face crumples in a million, deep lines. His chest rises sharply, and he tears the blindfold away from his face. "Jules! How—What—When—"

Cole devours me with one look and dismisses Trent with a brisk hand motion. "That'll be all, Darkwood."

"Are you fucking kidding me?" The vampire dashes closer and clutches my hands. His eyes pulse with questions. "Where were you? Why did my dad tell everyone you were dead?"

"He stabbed me, so maybe he genuinely thought I was." Sarcasm rolls off my tongue, but I'm shaken. Why is Trent in Faerie, apparently working for Cole?

"I can't believe—I'm so glad to see you, Jules. I made so many mistakes. I thought I had to become one of them. I knew how my dad was, yet I let him rule my life. Jules, you have to know—"

"You're dismissed, Darkwood."

"Wait a minute." Trent presses a hand to his chest. "Does this mean I'm free?"

Cole cranes his neck around, his body still stiff between Trent and me, shielding most of me from view. "We'll revisit your sentence later. Leave us."

"Sentence?" I cry out in surprise.

A suffocating wave of magic spices the air as Cole snaps, "I won't ask again."

Trent hustles out, his face ashen.

I raise a brow. "Now that we've established a bit more trust, can you explain what the fuck is going on? Why is Trent here, what happened?"

Cole rakes a hand through his curls, and the weight of his silence unnerves me.

"Will you at least unbind my powers?" I motion to the cuffs.

"No."

"Why not?"

He inches closer ever so slightly, surveilling me like a bird of prey watches the juicy little mouse he plans to tear to pieces for dinner. "You're supposed to be dead."

I tilt my head to the side. "I'm obviously not."

Cole tightens one fist around the hem of my towel, and his arm shakes. He looks about to tear the fabric off me and punish me for all the pain he endured, his jaw sets in the hardest line it has ever known.

I can see him calculating the fastest way to get inside me, and how desperate and rough it'd be.

I swallow a gasp, my skin still prickling from the heat of the bath, but I want him—*need* him to touch me, to make me his again and erase the years between us.

Before I can move, his hungry gaze suddenly flies to the corner of the room, and the restless energy between us wavers. "Get dressed. We're going back to Mellen."

10

BLACK AND WHITE

Allie

"Eleven years?" My heart jumps in my throat. Lydia's news acts as fresh snow, the shock of her explanation slowly sinking deep in my skin, both cold and numbing.

"Give or take." The seer motions for me to sit in the chair in front of her desk.

The library was reworked into cubicle-styles workspaces. Paint brushes, acrylics tubes, glasses of tainted water, wood-carving instruments, and a chessboard clutter her desk. The chandelier flickers above our heads, but old Pembrooke is nowhere to be seen.

I watch Lydia again. The roundness of her cheeks betrays not one inch of a wrinkle.

"Why didn't you age?" Goosebumps scatter on my arms, and I wrap them around my frame, feeling smaller than I have in a long time.

She smacks her lips. "I stayed here, in Dark Falls, to help Rose with research and force fields. We're the only ones who can see the hollows. The time in Dark Falls now goes by slower than anywhere else on earth."

I wiggle on the seat. "What happened?"

"An earthquake rocked the school the night you disappeared, and Darkwood told everyone you'd died. Dark Falls sank into a timesink—that's what we call the slow time zones. Hollows wormed their way inside the realm through the crater that was formed at the epicenter, so the Magisterium erected force fields around it and closed down the school."

I grip my forehead, trying to process.

A dry snicker grates her throat as she declutters her desk, arranging her instruments and brushes into a straight line. "We're actually going to open again for the Saturnalia quarter this year. That'll be another world of disaster. Darkwood apparently found a way to strengthen the barrier spell and trap the hollows, but I'm sure he's up to no good." She pauses on a deep sigh before she continues her explanation. "The veil between Earth and Faerie also thinned near the crater, so Cole ordered his men to patrol the borders in case another tectonic shift sends hollows directly into his kingdom."

My eyes widen. "You're speaking as though Cole is..."

"King of Faerie? Yes. Kirkan died in battle a couple of years after you disappeared." She picks up a paintbrush and dips it into black paint.

"Fucking hell." I eye the black, shadowy figurine in her hands. "I didn't know you played chess—or carved wood."

She plays with the end of her red braid. "I don't. I just had this... compulsion to make this set."

I take a closer look at the board. "Wait, this is Dark Falls."

The checkered squares have been painted with the Academy's colors, and the shape of the school crest—a raven with a feather in its talons—creates a shadow on the board. The pieces all ring a bell.

On the white side, the king has a long, pointy beard, and a splash of blood colors his mouth. The resemblance to Theodore Darkwood is spot on. The queen's long yellow cape and blond hair steal my breath. "My mother...is she alive?" I swallow hard, bracing myself for impact.

The seer doesn't glance up from her work. "Yes, of course. Why wouldn't she be?"

An audible gasp tears my throat. "Wait...she's alright?"

"Yes. She inspected us a week ago—with her usual charm, I might add," the redhead grumbles, sarcasm thick in her voice.

"I know you don't like me, Hawks, but this is a lot to take in. You're basically telling me I missed a decade of my life."

"It wasn't that long for me, either." A tightness at the corner of her mouth tells me she's annoyed with me again, the joy of the *Winslows-are-alive* news slowly eroding in the face of all my questions.

I don't care. I need answers, and time to process them.

"Where am I?" I skim the pieces for a blond woman. "I'd be a stupid white pawn, I guess." The line of white pawns glares back at me, one of them with blue hair and a half-buzzed cut. Olson.

She spares me a wistful look. "You're not on the board, yet."

"Mm."

The blacks have a king, too, with my sister's effigy. Her hair is thick with purple highlights, but she's definitely the king. Fire forms a halo above her head. And the queen on this side is...Cole, I realize. The dark ringlets and the wings leave no room for interpretation.

I point at the two pieces. "Shouldn't it be the other way around?"

"Why?" Her brush pauses in mid-air. "The queen protects the king. And as long as the king is safe, this side—" she motions to the black side of the chess board—"can win."

"But you thought Jules was dead."

"Actually, I was the only one who came to think she wasn't, but my powers scarcely make sense, so no one would believe me."

I touch the pieces one by one. A few of them, I don't recognize, but Deveraux is there, a tower for the blacks, and I find Dad, Lydia, Onyx —even Trent—standing on Jule's side.

If Jules was taken by the Fae patrol as Lydia suggested, she needs my help. I can't afford to spiral, but I can't help but pick up Daniel's piece.

The golden-red dragon stands in the space of a white knight, and I hold back a nervous cackle. Daniel's not a knight, but in the game of political chess, he's certainly a powerful, elusive piece. His moves are certainly not as predictable as the others. Two unicorns form the knights on the blacks' side.

"Where is Daniel—I mean Oz? Is he still headmaster?"

"Your two-faced ex is at a party tonight." She bites her bottom lip, the silence between us stretching into awkwardness until her gaze meets mine, her tone an octave lower than it was before. "It's actually his engagement party."

I dig my nails into the table, my whole body stiff. "Engagement to whom?" If a decade passed since I "died," I shouldn't be surprised, but electricity sparks in my hair.

Lydia picks up one of the white tower piece, a woman with brown hair and blood splatters that taint her white dress, and angles it to me. "Melanie Darkwood."

11

FIRE AND THORNS

Allie

*A*nts of thunder crawl along my arms. A dark cloud quite literally follows my every move. All those days on the boat, holding my frustrations in, and now I'm...unleashed. Unhinged. I want to shatter Oz with a lightning rod, expose him for the liar that he is, and dance over his ashes.

Lydia seems oblivious to my fury—or eager to change the subject. "If Jules was taken by the Fae, Flynn will contact us soon."

The mention of the obnoxiously beautiful, maverick Fae intrudes on my thoughts, more sudden and unsettling than a bee sting. "Flynn?"

"He helps us with the force fields to contain the hollows here so they don't slip into Faerie. We trade information," Lydia explains.

"Excuse me if I'm not on board with leaving my sister's fate in

Flynn Verinos' hands." Disbelief thick in my voice, I give her the stink eye.

Deveraux clears her throat loudly behind me, luring me away from the puddle of regrets and humiliation threatening to drown me like quicksand.

I crane my neck around to look at my professor and almost topple over.

Barron stares up at the suspended chandelier with a puzzled expression on his face. With his arms crossed over his broad chest, he looks gigantic.

I grip the back of my chair. "What are you doing here?"

He doesn't look away from the ceiling, tilting his head from one side to the other like he can't quite understand how the physics of wax and fire work. "Rose invited me."

Rose?

"You said you wanted nothing to do with Dark Falls," I argue, my palms suddenly sweaty as hell. Barron was a lot to take in on his boat, but here...I might never look away. How a man can look so intimidating wearing only jeans and a monochrome t-shirt is beyond me, but he does. His green-freckled gaze bears into me as though he can read my thoughts, like my pain is nothing but a crown I wear as an artifice.

He raises his hand to the flames. The warm light of the candles grows a shade darker—almost purple. "I changed my mind," he says quietly.

I don't know how, but his call echoes in my bones, the very marrow chanting for me to get closer to him. The dark thoughts I was plagued with a minute ago are gone, replaced by the incomparable need to touch him.

Lydia leans in, her elbows propped over the chess board. "Who is *that?*"

"No one," I whisper back.

The legs of the chair screech on the linoleum as I stand up. "You shouldn't—"

Deveraux obscures Barron's frame from my vision, freeing me

from the unnatural, hypnotic hold. "Your father went looking for the unicorns. He thought we could never fix Dark Falls—or the realm—without their help. I disagreed with his plan, but now…I think he was right."

She lifts her chin up at the sailor. "If we want to find Robert, we need a way through the mists. Mr. Barron here can lead us through them."

Barron threads closer to me. "Ye can imagine I won't find my brother in Miami as planned, so my schedule…freed up." He extends his hand to Lydia. "I'm Kayde Barron."

The redhead gapes. "Lydia Hawks."

They shake hands, and the Scot's gaze softens. "Yer grandmother was a close friend of mine. She was born in Scotland, did ye know? Her powers were unparalleled."

Lydia nods, and her forehead wrinkles before she reaches for Barron's arm. "Those are blakkr naetrelding marks." She runs her hands over the skin of his left forearm before suddenly letting him go. "Shit, I'm sorry. I didn't mean to touch you like that."

A quick smile ghosts over the sailor's lips. "No harm done, *Lydia*. Ye lek exactly like her, did ye know?" The deep, sexual way he ushers the words irks my temper.

Close friend my ass.

A deep shade of red settles in the hollow of Lydia's chest.

I cross my arms. "You could have warned us the time had passed quicker out here." Whatever magic he used on me before has waned, but I'm still deeply unnerved by the phenomenon.

Barron continues to scrutinize Lydia with the most unabashed interest as he answers, "We sailed through a tempest, so it could have gone either way. Either you were gone for ten years—or ten minutes."

I click my tongue. "Well, a head's up would have been nice."

The seer jolts to her senses. "Well…I'll check the woods in case Flynn managed to leave me a message."

Rose hands Barron a steaming cup of coffee. "And I'll see what I can offer you in exchange for your services, Mr. Barron."

The two women hustle out, leaving me alone with the Scot and his clearly vivid recollection of all the sex he had with Lydia's grandmother.

My heart races as I walk to the stacks of books near Lydia's desk and run my fingers along the spines. Most of them are ancient tomes, and I read the titles, looking for anything else to occupy my mind. History of the Three Realms. Lessons from Demons. An Underworld Lie. Undead Connection. The Phoenix Songs. Pazar's Bestiary.

I slide the last one from the shelf and fan the pages, looking for a page marker or hand-written notes, but the sight of the dragon on the cover pulls my mind down a dark, rabbit hole.

The heat of his breath brushes my neck. "Don't let it destroy ye."

I spin around to face him, spooked by his closeness. I didn't even see him move. The tremble of power wafts through the library once more in a nefarious shroud. "What?"

"Whoever he is. He's not worth it. Believe me." His gaze slews to my lips, and he leans down.

"How dare you—" I move to slap his cheek.

He catches my wrist mid-swing, his calloused thumb on my pulse point. "Yer fury sizzles. Yer pain suffocates. The taste of it is so thick, I can't think."

The compulsion to reach for him is undeniable, my arms shake in restraint, and my brain finally catches up with what's happening. "You're a vengeance demon?"

He slides his thumb up to my palm, his long fingers curled around my knuckles. "A druid, a warlock, a sorcerer...I was born on earth. I'm like you, lass. With less self-importance, a wee bit more sense, and a ton more experience."

"Fuck you." I wrench my hand away. "You're no warlock. You're immortal."

His soft chuckle caresses my cheek, "Like I said, I'm a druid. We do things a bit differently."

"You sell your soul for power, you mean?"

His gaze sharpens with a dangerous, but inviting, edge. "I can take ye through the mists to find your dad. If ye want."

"Right... And what do you want in return?" I ask.

A crossroad devil always bargains for better than he's due. My father used to tell us tales about the Underworld. Now that I know he really went there, I figure they were more than children's stories meant to keep us in line.

The Scot's Adam's apple bobs. "Let me taste ye."

I shouldn't.

But his proximity flips my stomach, and electricity buzzes through my veins.

He strokes the side of my face with his rough thumb. "Feed me your rage, lass. Let me ease yer soul."

I crush my mouth to his, a kiss a simple price to pay to dry up the well of self-loathing imprisoning me.

Every single brush of his tongue soothes me.

After a few seconds in his arms, I can *remember* why I'm ruined, but I can no longer *feel* it. Barron delivers me from myself with his corruptive peace, and I sink my nails into his neck, eager to find out how much solace his wicked mouth can bring.

He tastes of cloves and cinnamon. Ash and fire and thorns.

A squeeze in my belly softens my knees, but Barron catches my fall, his large hands gripping my waist with a ferocity that unravels me. I slip my fingers under his cotton shirt, eager to feel the ridges and grooves of his chest. His tattoos buzz with energy, and the ink smudges under my fingers, cool and fresh.

I tear myself away and press the back of my hand over my bruised lips. "You're a pain junky."

"Maybe." His chest rises and falls, his eyes unfocused as though he's high from whatever he stole from me.

A tattoo moves on his chest, shaped like a black cat. "Is that—"

"Mal wanted to come along. Apparently, she can take any shape here, so I decided to...carry her around."

I stare at the bouncing cat, totally weirded out. Did she see us kiss?

"Hey, Mal," I greet her awkwardly.

The ink shimmers in response.

"That damn curse...if only I could find out who wove it." Barron presses his lips together.

"What happened to her? Why was she cursed?" I ask.

"After her mother died, me and me brother raised her. That was a long time ago, before the hollows took over the small island where ye and I met, but I better not get into the details."

I cross my arms. "What about the mists? What are they?

"The mists are a passage to the nether planes."

The name rings a bell. Dad used to leave for the nether planes for weeks at a time.

"And this passage is close by?"

"The mists are accessed with a spell—not geography," Barron explains. "It's a land outside the three realms...some say a remnant of a fourth realm that was destroyed long ago. The old saying is that anyone traveling through the mists cannot hope to return without leaving something old behind or carrying something new."

"Which is flowery language for what, exactly?" The ancient texts make everything sound fancy and mystical, but what Barron is saying sounds like a simple transaction.

The corners of his mouth twitch. "I guess we'll find out."

12

TALE AS OLD AS TIME

Jules

The Fae sunrise looms under the horizon, blood-orange clouds stretching above our heads. We rode for hours in the dark, and my body is numb from the strain of the saddle and the coldness of Cole's welcome. He hasn't uttered a single word to me since we left his war tent and barely glanced my way.

Instead, he shouts command after command to his *assistant,* our chaperone, the tight-lipped sprite, Jameson.

The sprite and his king ride a few paces behind me. They are discussing the ins and outs of some skirmish between two generals, and the aftershock of our reunion prevents me from interrupting.

Hooves beat the path and lull me into a dreamlike state, my mind still trying to reconcile my quick trip to the Underworld, to the Faerie time-jump and this new reality.

This new Cole.

He made me wear a soldier's tunic and hood to hide my identity, as though the whole realm might collapse with word of my non-death.

When we get to the palace, Cole finally speaks. "Let's clean-up and settle in. We'll have breakfast in an hour. We can talk then." He throws his horse's bridle over the pummel and strokes its neck.

Normally, I'd be eager to push his buttons and demand answers, be my hot-tempered self, but the lost decade instills an eerie sense of patience and dread. He still won't look at me, but breakfast sounds a hell of a lot nicer than his frosty behavior on the ride here, so I nod. "Okay."

The interlude might give me time to face my new reality.

Jameson's leathery wings flap impatiently behind him as he escorts me to Cole's room. The palace hasn't changed much, but Cole's bedroom is sterile, the shelves behind the big bed empty, and dust hangs in the air. Clearly, no one has stepped foot in this room for *months*.

"Cole doesn't sleep here anymore, does he?" I ask. He must have moved to the King's quarters, a section of the palace I never visited before.

Jameson opens the curtains wide, the view of the city reassuring in its familiarity. "He asked for you to be placed here regardless."

A fake, sugary smile glazes my lips. "Mmm. I'm not an object to be *placed* anywhere, and I'd like to see his real bedroom."

The professional, all-business exterior of the sprite doesn't relent at my cheekiness. "You'll meet the king in his quarters soon enough. I'll send Mary to you, but no one other than her is to learn of your return."

"Why not?"

"Your highness," Jameson bows, his neck stiff, before he hustles out.

I trace the silk black pillows with my fingers.

I can be reasonable. I have no clue what happened in Faerie or what new threats arose in my absence. An hour is tolerable enough, but I'll get to the bottom of this. Maybe Cole wants us to reunite here for good reasons, and with some luck, he'll explain everything when we're alone.

But a sour, hollow current in my blood tells me something is wrong, beyond the simple passage of time and highly charged revelations. The lingering taste of Cole's desperate kiss is about the only thing keeping me sane.

What if Jameson couldn't take me to Cole's quarters because someone else lives there? What if Cole avoided my questions because Flynn is dead?

How am I supposed to accept all these changes?

If the world has moved on, thinking I was buried six feet underground, how can I accomplish all that I set out to do, bring justice to Beth, and expose Oz and Darkwood? Have I been gone so long that I've become irrelevant?

Fire stings my chest, my emotions burning hotter and wilder than I need them to, and I paw at the empty space in the valley between my breasts where my emerald pendant usually sits. There's not much to do in the sterile room, so I lie down on the bed, wishing Cole—*my* Cole—was here with me, and doze off.

"You're back." Mary looks down her nose at me as I jolt awake. Her high cheekbones are sharper than before, but her snobbish attitude hasn't changed.

A wry smile curls my lips. "How disappointing for you."

"Get dressed, the King is ready."

Ohhh—the King is ready, is he?

Rebellion spreads to my blood, and fire lurks underneath my skin.

The Fae servant has laid down a black dress on the bed, and I graze the textured corset, the laced neckline so plunging my throat dries up. "Can I wear something else?"

She clicks her tongue. "He's grieved for you for *years*. What you wear doesn't matter."

I bite my tongue. "Alright, but take these damn cuffs off!"

Mary reaches inside her pockets for a small key and complies with a click of the tongue. I rub my wrists in relief, but the spell attached to the shackles doesn't dissipate.

Fuck it. Dress or no dress, the entire vibe is plain *wrong*. The only right thing about it is my emerald necklace, which waits for me next to the dress. I let out a relieved sigh as I secure it back around my neck.

The laced hem of the dress waves at my mid-thigh, the scratch of the fabric maddening, and I hate how my thin frame makes me look even younger than I am.

I follow Mary to an uncharted part of the palace. The decorative metallic foliage grows sparse as we reach a long corridor flanked by tall windows. A breath-taking view of Faerie's sacred tree, the Hawthorn, leaves me no doubt we're heading up to the King's wing.

We pass another set of golden doors and enter a dining room. Cole sits at one end of a ginormous banquet table, but he doesn't get up as we arrive. The setup is grand and ludicrous. Freshly cooked meat and acidic wine flavor the air, but my stomach clenches.

"Where should we start?" I ask, my attitude tucked away by the seriousness on Cole's face. Despite his icy behavior, I feel for him. I don't know what I would have done in his position, if I'd lost him only to find him again a decade later...

He serves himself a glass of wine, his eyes locked on his golden cup. "You go."

Alright, I can give him this. I walk to the opposite end of the table where the only other chair awaits, and sit. "After I almost closed down the tear, Darkwood double-crossed me and sank a dagger in my guts. Allie intervened and tried to fight him off, Onyx too, but he had this magic armor around him, so Allie flew us into the Underworld portal instead."

Cole links his hands together in front of his face, listening intently.

"There was a huge building on the other side, but it was in ruins and full of hollows, so we had to flee. The dagger wound healed— thanks to you."

I recount our weeks at sea and the naga attack, giving as much detail as I can until I get to Barron's claim about the Underworld hub. Cole glowers from the other side of the room, a dark cloud stuck to his face.

"It confirms what you thought—that the Unseelie are using the Underworld hub as a way to travel from Faerie back to their lair. Barron said—"

Cole squints. "Who's Barron? He just happened to be walking by the Underworld tear when you crashed through it?"

I nod. "Mallory knew him, but he wasn't very open about his past with us. I'm sure he had something to hide."

"And Mallory is—"

"Onyx, yes." The conversation still rings like an interrogation.

He tilts his head to one side.

I force a deep breath down my lungs. "Is Flynn okay?"

He grows a shade whiter. "Verinos is no longer my concern—or yours."

What the fuck?

The backward answer evaporates what was left of my goodwill and patience, so I slam the utensils on the table and jerk to my feet. "What is wrong with you? Why won't you touch me? Why do you speak to me as though I'm a stranger in an interrogation room? Why are we sitting on opposite ends of an enormous table full of food when we're clearly not fucking hungry?"

He rubs down his face with both hands. "You're exactly the same... rash and hot-tempered."

"Ohh—*I'm* the problem here?" I rush over to him, hating how withdrawn he appears, how cold. "You checked to see if I was truly Jules... I might argue you're not really Cole."

He shrugs—fucking *shrugs*—and discards his napkin. "I changed."

"Not for the better," I croak, my jaw clenched so hard, it hurts.

"Were you always this impatient?"

"When did you stop being smart?

Our gaze locks. Red freckles shine in his amber eyes, and the wave of emotions really, really...turns me on. I want to crush my mouth to his until his face shows something besides arrogance. I want a glimpse of the Cole from the war tent, the one that looked like he was about to throw me to the ground and make me his again.

I *need* him.

I inch forward slowly, the way you would approach frightened prey, without breaking the spell. He digs his nails into the armrest of the chair, nostrils flaring as though he's fighting with himself.

I take advantage of his indecision to close the gap between us and straddle him, one hand laying flat on his chest, the other slipping up to his neck to caress his short curls. "We can fight all day, but what's the use? I missed you—and I was only gone a few weeks. I can't imagine what it was like for you."

The kiss is tentative at first. Fae wine lingers on his tongue, and the spicy scent of his cologne melts my insides. He encircles my waist, the warm planes of his chest tightly pressed against me. I sigh out a relieved breath. This is *better.*

We rediscover each other with each languid stroke, until Cole jerks to his feet, taking me along with him, my thighs wrapped around his midriff. My ass hits the table before he devours my neck, his lips both hard and soft on my pulse point.

The new shape of his arms is sinfully hot—if not a bit intimidating.

He squeezes the soft flesh of my thighs, spreading them open. His scars gleam under the torches' light. I want to memorize them and ease into this new version of him, whereas Cole is clearly aiming for *fast and rough.* I could have gotten on board with that if he'd looked at me, but a sense of doom hovers in my belly.

His eyes are screwed shut, and it's messy. I need reassurance that he's opening up, not merely fucking me out of his mind.

"Cole, look at me," I breathe against his chest.

He abruptly pulls away, gripping his hair. "You're still so...young."

There's so much hate in the word, it sparks a fire storm in my chest.

"You're too old for me now? Too worldly for an eighteen-year-old?" A hot line of anger lances up my spine. If it wasn't for the scars and the frost in his amber eyes, he'd look exactly the same, too. I lift my chin up. "What's a decade to you?"

"Everything," he snarls. "I might be immortal, but I was nineteen then. A child. I had no idea what I was doing."

I slide my butt past the ledge of the table to stand.

Cole paces the room back and forth. "Losing you once showed me what a weakness love is."

"So losing me twice is the answer?" I press hard on my forehead, trying to follow his damn logic, and fail. There must be something he isn't telling me, something gnawing at him for him to act so...volatile.

His gaze snaps to mine, and his whole body shakes with rage as though my question is the ultimate sacrilege. "I'm not *losing* you again. You'll stay right here, so I can keep an eye on you."

My brows furrow. "Here, as in Faerie?"

"Here, as in my rooms." He heads toward the exit, and for every step, my heart pounds harder.

A mass of stone sinks in my belly, and my head starts to shake in denial. I need to go home and compare notes with Allie, figure this shit out before I explode into an endless ball of tears. This whole time dilation situation is an absolute nightmare.

"I can't just stay here while you accept my existence. Allie is waiting for me back in Dark Falls!" I shout at Cole's retreating back.

"I waited eleven years. Your sister can wait a little longer." The door closes behind him, and the sound echoes inside my cells.

13

THE BLOND FAE

Jules

The King's apartments in which Cole *imprisoned* me include a bedroom, bathroom, dining room, office, and library. After his tantrum, I tried to follow him, but a spell prevented me from opening the doors. In the absence of the right ingredients and gear to thwart the powerful Fae magic that seals these rooms, my attempts to dispel the barrier were fruitless, and I haven't been desperate enough to try and break the windows, yet.

I read every letter on Cole's desk to catch up with the politics of Faerie and fell asleep on his bed at the crack of dawn. The next afternoon, I arranged all the documents I could find into three piles. The bad-news-about-Unseelie pile, the intra-realm-unrest in another, and the shit-is-hitting-the-fan-with-Earth documents.

I thought Cole would cool off and return after a reasonable amount of time, but my patience is wearing thin. Although…knowing how much shit he has to deal with cools my temper.

As the red Fae sun descends past the castle walls, Mary clicks her tongue to get my attention. "Here's your dinner." The Fae servant sneaks in and out of my prison as though the spell doesn't apply to her.

"This is the fifth meal you've brought me today," I answer without looking.

"You've barely eaten."

"I'm not hungry." The loud creasing of parchment echoes in the silent room as I leaf through the letters again, arranging them into chronological order.

"You're too thin," Mary says on a reproachful sigh. "Stop sulking and eat."

She's not wrong, but despite what she thinks, I haven't fasted to spite her. My stomach is still queasy as hell, spooked by the sudden abundance of delicious and greasy proteins.

I lean into her false hypothesis. "If Cole wants to fatten me up, all he has to do is release me." Maybe if Cole hears that I'm too stubborn to eat, he'll deign to visit, and I can kick his ass for sequestering me in his damn magic palace.

Mary leaves without another word, and I return to my work.

A letter from Darkwood demanding the return of the unicorn horn brings a feverish heat to my neck. Gods…Allie and I are just starting to mend fences. If her mother died while we were away, she'll blame me.

The relations between the High Council and Cole are tense as hell, and I can't help but think he imprisoned me in his rooms on purpose, expecting me to snoop through all those papers.

But then, why wouldn't he just say so?

About an hour later, a quiet knock on the door jerks me out of my investigation, and I peel myself from the floor, the papers I still need to read scattered across the red carpet of the office.

I inch open the door, hoping to find Cole on the other side, and my blood freezes. "Brie?"

Bright green hair waves down one side of the mermaid's face, the other side buzzed close to the scalp. The haircut gives her an edge, her preppy days behind her. A short black cloak embroidered with silver and copper accents covers her shoulders, and a black skirt highlights her long legs.

"Fuck," she croaks. "It's really you." Her face hasn't aged a day, but she stares me up and down as though she can't quite believe what she's seeing.

"What are you—"

She hands me a bland, gray cloak, with sleeves and a large hood, similar to the one Jameson had me wear on my ride over here. "Put this on."

I bite my bottom lip and consider her offering.

"Do you really want to spend the next year locked inside the castle?" she asks.

I reluctantly slip on the cloak. "No."

"Then hurry. We have a short window to get you out."

"We?"

She ignores my question, and I follow her down the long hallway that offers a fantastic view of the interior courtyard and the sacred Hawthorn tree. The Fae moon burns in the night sky and brightens the silver lines of Brie's ensemble. Her tailored clothes match Cole's to a frightening degree, and my heart just about leaps out of my chest.

Of all the people Cole could have turned to after my "death,"— besides Flynn of course—Brie makes the most sense, and yet, it hurts. Eleven years...

While my brain understands it's a long time to remain single, my heart rebels. It thuds angrily in my throat, and I dig my heels in the ground. "Are you and Cole..."

She motions me along. "Someone had to clean up your mess."

My eyes narrow at her peculiar choice of words. "What does that mean?"

She yanks my hood over my hair. "Don't ask too many questions, and you will sleep better for it." Her boots clank on the marble as she guides me to a servant's stairwell.

Torches flicker on the walls, and the scent of dust and mildew dries my mouth as we trek deeper into the castle. Is she only freeing me because she wants me gone?

"The capital's brothel hosts a poker game tonight. Flynn always attends when he's on leave. He'll catch you up on the latest developments."

The mention of Flynn uncoils my muscles, and I pick up the pace. We weave through the secret passageways underneath the palace, and Brie appears to be more than familiar with the maze of tunnels.

Stupidly, I check her fingers for a ring, but I know Fae don't use them. Long, triangular sleeves run past her wrists and hide a potential Fae-wedding scar.

A bitter pout glazes her red lips as she catches me staring. She opens a solid door at the top of a narrow stairwell, and we emerge inside a tiny, dark room.

A lattice window opens to a darkened street where paved stones glisten with rain under a lonely lamppost. A small desk, unlit candles, and ledgers furnish the small space, this secret entrance somehow disguised as a tiny office.

Brie holds open the door. "Here you go. I can't be seen here, but Verinos should be easy to find."

"Are you kidding? You just said this is a *brothel*." I search her face for the truth, but my witchy-instincts are quiet.

"Strip club would be more accurate." She points to a leather bag sitting atop a wooden chair in the corner. "You should change. Your black dress isn't exactly nondescript. There's enough money in that bag to buy your passage to Earth if Verinos is too drunk to bother, and the power-binding spell they put on you should wear off in a few hours."

I switch my weight from one foot to the other, stuck in place, indecision gnawing my insides. She certainly got her black ducks in a row to make sure I'd agree to leave.

"The Cole you knew is gone, Winslow. Whatever fragments of him remain…you should walk away." An equal dose of contempt and fear mingle on her breath.

"Because you're with him now," I say, testing my theory.

"I said what I said. Make of it what you will."

I swallow hard. "I love him."

Her incensed mermaid gaze freezes my blood. "So do I."

I'm not sure I should have followed Brie out of the palace. A big part of me wants to stay and force the issue with Cole, but the prospect of getting some agency back after the unpleasant, and frankly traumatizing, kidnapping experience is too appealing. I need time and space to make sense of it all.

I'm not ready for her to tell me Cole remarried.

I'll never be ready, so I dash forward and grip the bag. "I will go for now, but don't think it means I've given up."

Brie spares us the torture of awkward goodbyes and leaves, the door closing quietly behind her, melding with the wall with no knob or any visual cue to its presence. I close my eyes, trying to sense if it's protected by a spell of some kind, but detect no trace of magic. With shaky fingers, I rummage through the bag, relieved to find everything she mentioned and also a few key ingredients for basic spells. A bag of Fae coins rustles at the bottom of the satchel.

The clothes she left me are Fae-made, but they look more like Earth fashion than the traditional tunics. The long-sleeved v-neck shirt hugs my curves, and the comfortable pants are high-waisted. The dark gray wool sweater has a hoodie to hide my hair. I stuff the discarded dress in the bag and throw it over my shoulder.

Voices, laughs, and the clanks of glass on glass seep inside the antechamber. The door in front of me shows no crack of light or doorknob, so I push out of the small office. Inching forward, I peek at the other side. I'm halfway down a secluded hallway leading to a series of unmarked doors. Heated moans rise from the depths of the hall-way, but I quickly adjust the hood over my hair and head toward the bustle of the main room in search of a familiar head of blond hair.

A two-story club stretches in front of me, with a stage and mezzanine. Red curtains mask the stage's depth, and to my relief, most people are just drinking and gambling.

Members of the staff—both male and female mortals—pass around trays of food and drinks. Scarves and jewels are tied in strategic places, embellishing their nakedness, and a crimson blush covers my cheeks. I've never been to a brothel—or a strip club.

Most of the patrons are upstairs, so I climb to the mezzanine, my sweaty fingers gliding along the mahogany banister.

A dark-haired waiter crosses my path at the top of the staircase. "Welcome to the Lion's Pub. Do you need anything, luv?"

Jaw slightly askew, I try not to notice the huge bulge in his Fae-made boxers. "I'm looking for Flynn Verinos?"

A soft purr whistles out of the man's mouth. "He's upstairs, in the back."

"Thanks." I scratch the inside of my lower arm nervously.

My heartbeat spikes.

What if he's not the Flynn I remember? What if he's fucking someone else *right now?*

A wave of anxiety engulfs me as Flynn comes into view, but to my relief, he looks exactly the same. If scars blackened his heart in my absence, not one inch of his face shows off the wear. His blond hair is long enough to be messy, the golden locks tousled in a perfectly imperfect way. A boyish smile warms his face as he plays cards. The congenial cockiness with which he wipes his winnings toward him is so totally him…my heart bleeds.

Who would have imagined I would be so glad to find Flynn Verinos unchanged, about to fleece a poor bloke from his money— and dignity.

Our gazes lock over the pile of coins, and his ocean-blue eyes widen. The bustle of the waiters, the rhythmic taps of the cards against the tables, everything dies down to a mere whisper.

My chest expands and contracts.

Flynn flies off his seat, and his chair topples over. He swallows one last swig of beer and dumps his mug on an empty table as he weaves his way through the crowd, his eyes never leaving mine, full of questions and doubts.

The dagger strapped to his side catches the light, but he doesn't reach for his weapon. Instead, he plants both hands around my face and pulls me in for a kiss.

His tongue asks questions mine can't answer. The soft, sensual brushes rip away my armor, one delicious lick at a time, and by the time he draws back, I'm shaking.

The blue depths of his eyes shine with tears. "It's really you."

A small breath whizzes out of my lungs. "Even Cole couldn't tell that fast."

"Cole has a giant sword stuck up his ass. He couldn't tell someone who loves him from a rock."

A low, teary giggle escapes me.

Flynn captures my hand in his, and the pressure of his grasp cuts the blood supply to my fingers, but I don't mind. "Come with me, witch. You have a lot to explain."

A bittersweet ache pulses in my throat. As happy as I am for this reunion to be more "let's catch up" and less "bondage," I'm...disappointed. It's unfair, but I wish Cole had acted the same way, and Flynn's positive response only solidifies all the rotten ways Cole treated me. His warm welcome highlights the flaws in my husband better than a troll holds a club.

He ushers me to a private table tucked in the corner. I scoot close to him in the half-crescent booth, unable to let go. "What happened between you two?"

"Let's drink." He orders a pitcher of beer.

I tug on his hand. "Flynn!"

"Let's not talk about him. Let's talk about you. Are you this young and beautiful because of your newfound immortality, or did the Underworld swallow you whole and spit you back out in a different timeline?"

I grin at the stupid compliment, but really, it's the total lack of change to his obnoxiously loud personality that gets me. "I was gone a month, tops. I heard you lived through a decade...I can't imagine—"

He brings a hand to his chest. "Ouch. I'm not that old. About four years for me, thank you."

I let out a sigh of relief. Maybe that explains the difference between him and Cole...Maybe there's hope for the Fae King.

I swallow a long swig of beer, the wheat bitter on my tongue, but I'd drink a thousand beers with Flynn. For me, it's only been weeks since we...My cheeks heat up at the memory, but I force my brain back on the most pressing matter. "What happened to Dark Falls?"

Flynn leans in for a kiss, but I smack two fingers over his mouth. "I need to know."

He groans like a kid being refused a stick of candy and sighs. "Dark Falls has...sunk. The barrier between the three realms thinned, a rift opened, and the territories around it sledged inside an abyss of time. A timesink the size of a city took hold of it, and anything that gets too close to Dark Falls' center remains almost suspended in time. Your lot isn't used to dealing with the contraction and dilation of timelines. Freaks the earthlings out. Volunteers guard the walls and refresh the spells to contain the hollows, but it's not good, Jules. Not good at all. Darkwood declared a state of emergency, and he's basically calling all the shots."

He swallows another mouthful of beer. "On Faerie's side, the barriers are stronger, but we have the Unseelie banging down our doors...we're stretched thin, and after Kirkan died—"

"How did he die?"

Flynn pouts as though he swallowed a mouthful of fermented fish. "Unseelie attack. Cole barely made it out. The healers couldn't fix him right away, so for a few days, he hung between life and death. Without him, there was no clear succession. His siblings aren't good politicians, most of them too caught up in their luxuries and pleasures to give it up. Darkwood called for a Seelie government and the end of monarchy, which would have weakened our magic. He almost succeeded, too, but Cole pulled through, and here we are."

I grab my head, overwhelmed by the torrent of news.

He inches closer, the heat of his body delicious. "I'm on leave, but when I'm not here, I'm guarding the Dark Falls' barrier. Cole posted me there not to have to deal with me anymore. That's why so little time passed for me, too."

The weariness of the last few days condenses into exhaustion. I need to return to Allie and unscramble all of this. "Take me back to the Academy," I ask Flynn.

He pulls my wrist to him and kisses it with reverence. "Anything for my queen. But first, I need to show you something."

14

LEGENDS

Allie

"Where is your biggest mirror?" Barron asks Deveraux. The multi-story library seems smaller with him in it.

"We have a dedicated room to travel to the nether realm," the professor answers. "If you're going through the mists, I'm coming with you."

Lydia's eyes dart to the golden clock on her desk every few seconds. "And I'll stay here, in case Jules returns."

Deveraux leads us under the main building, beyond the part of the basement that is used for Ancient Arts studies, a graduate-level class. A door with a triangular keyhole waits for us there. She picks the key out of the tight bun at the nape of her neck and twists it into the lock.

The door creaks open, revealing a...ballet studio? A horizontal bar runs the length of the room, its four walls completely covered with mirrors. The glossy white linoleum enhances the illusion of walking into an endless dream.

I narrow my eyes at the modern set-up, the sleek interior giving me major Magisterium vibes. "I feel like I should have worn my ballet slippers. Is this a portal?"

Barron snickers. "Not yet."

Deveraux arches a brow. "You're not wrong. This room doubled as a dance studio for a while."

The electrical light fixtures along the walls burst to life, and a dark, bluish light seeps through the air.

Barron slides a wavey dagger out of his belt and carves a deep cut into his palm.

He smudges the thumb from the opposite hand in his blood and walks to the reflective glass. With confident strokes, he draws a large circle on the mirror, then splits it in four equally-sized quarters, the pattern slowly forming a Celtic knot, the mesmerizing lines inter-woven with each other.

When it's done, he takes a step back and contemplates his work. Black ink spreads over his right hand as he raises it to the drawing.

"Hriga dyrr."

The now liquid surface of the mirror undulates, the mercury-like drops floating in mid-air, stretching and rearranging, ignoring the earthly laws of physics and fluid dynamics.

The Underworld tear didn't emit any sound, but I can hear a thou-sand tiny, discrete bells chime through the mirror. They...whisper to me—a promise and a warning.

Barron kicks off his shoes and motions for us to do the same. Deveraux had already unlaced her boots, so I quickly slip out of mine.

"After you," he says to Deveraux.

With a grumble, I close the march.

Instead of a cold sting, the portal coats my face and arms. A solid wave of silver washes over us until we emerge on the other side.

Heavy mists stick to the air, erasing most of my surroundings from view, including my companions. I can see my hands, but not much else.

"Professor?" I call out to the white void.

"Over here, Allison," Deveraux answers.

I cough out a wave of humidity and join her and Barron a few paces to my left.

Deveraux mutters an incantation under her breath, and sunshine pierces the shadows.

The patches of mist condense. Suspended droplets pepper my shoulders as Deveraux and Barron's silhouettes slice through the fog. A thin layer of water splashes between my bare toes, separating the warm sunbeams in colorful rainbows, and I gaze down at my reflection.

I squint, hints of the ballet studio visible below my feet, as though we're actually standing *over* the mirror we just walked *through*.

My brain strains to grasp the physics of the magic, and my reflection in the water spooks me. A bright yellow aura shines like a halo around my head—incredibly distracting and beautiful at the same time.

I gasp as Mallory's naked frame appears at the corner of my eyes. "Mal?"

She looks down at her hands, her breasts covered by her thick curls. "I'm me. How is that possible?"

"The mists reveal the true nature of people. Always." Rose shrugs off her long trench coat and offers it to Mallory. The demon wraps the black jacket around her frame. "Funny how both of you forgot to mention we had a demon in our midst..."

Blood heats my face and ears, but Barron only shrugs in response.

Shadows create a black, living force around him that absorbs all light, and he sticks out like a sore thumb in the white, silvery space. "Someone's already here."

Without warning, vines sprout from the ground and twist around our ankles and legs. I let out a high-pitched scream.

"Fuck, it's a trap," Mallory yelps, wrestling the sentient roots at her feet.

Thunder rumbles in my palms, but the stream of power only

excites them, and the ones I manage to snap off are quickly replaced by sturdier ones. They snake up to my midriff, immobilizing me.

"Don't fight them. It'll only make it worse," Rose says.

Lightning sparks off my skin and blackens a few twigs.

A longer, nasty-looking ivy slithers in my direction. The grope-y plant crawls along the skin of my arms, encircles my wrists, and binds them behind my back.

A slender, familiar silhouette stalks through the mist, and my heart pulses in my throat. A long white mane flows around the newcomer's face.

Now, I know what it feels like to look at the face of your mistakes. Sweat gathers at my temples, and my stomach churns. A heated wave of nausea threatens to floor me.

The only thing that sets this woman apart from Miss Eillis is her gaze. It's sharper, and full of secrets. Other than that, she's an exact copy of the woman I murdered. Her long, layered green gown is impervious to the silver water at our feet, and a long matching scarf covers her shoulders.

Deveraux wiggles in her restraints. "Thea."

"Rose..." The breathless name reverberates through the air, the surprise on the woman's face bordering on anguish. "You shouldn't have come."

"I had to."

The plants around Deveraux's ankles retreat, and she trembles as Thea pulls her into a bone-crushing hug. Despite her somber greeting, this clone of Elsbeth Eillis looks awfully happy to see her, and they linger in the embrace for a long, long time.

My throat itches.

Mallory plays with her fingers.

Beth's doppelgänger observes us over Deveraux's shoulder. "I'm Amalthea. I guard the gates to Nether Realms, a place as sacred as my people. As long as you are on my lands, you will surrender your powers. Do you agree?"

We all nod.

The woman stomps one foot on the ground. Tiny fireflies of magic glide along my arms and pool in my wrists. The warm, orange light forms shackles on my wrists, and the familiar itch of a binding spell scratches my spine.

Amalthea squints at Mallory. "You were cursed."

Barron steps off the surface of the fluid mirror and onto white sand. "Can you do something about it?"

The graceful, eerie unicorn clutches the long skirt of her dress and motions us along. "Come. My house is close by. We can talk there."

She guides us to a small cottage right on the beach. A string of white columns stretch along the covered porch. Mist hugs the garbled roof where a bronze rooster weathervane totters from side to side, the house literally covered in clouds, and I wonder if it's really there, or merely a dream.

A man slams open the door. "Peanut?"

My heart swells. "Dad!"

My father wrenches me in his bone-crushing embrace on Amalthea's porch. "Is it really you? Or is the magic of this place strong enough to turn ghosts into flesh."

His old-fashioned ensemble makes him look like a period-piece hero, his usual black jacket and red cape nowhere to be found. He also shaved his gray beard off, the polished look taking years off his face—or is it the magic of this place?

"It's really her," Thea confirms.

She and the others head inside the house to give us some privacy.

Dad observes Barron and Mallory in turn, but his focus quickly settles back on me.

"You look so different," I blurt out, not comprehending how—if a decade passed—my father managed to escape it.

"And your sister? Is she—" his voice cracks.

"She's in Faerie, but she's alive."

"Thank the Gods." He sobs in my arms, and I gently pat his back. "What happened?"

I recount the gist of our underworld visit, and Dad explains how Darkwood used the earthquake to explain both our deaths and the hollow invasion that followed. Of course, he didn't admit his part in it, and how he tried to murder me and my sister.

After a lengthy talk, we join the others in the living room. Potted plants hang from the ceiling in pots of different colors and shapes.

Amalthea invites us to sit on her colonial furniture and serves us tea, the whole scene straight from a period novel. Barron glares at the tea set like he's asking himself how much it would go for on the black market. Mallory perches on a faded-pink chair, picking at her cuticles.

"Robert insisted that I should join the fight, but my place is here," Thea says.

Rose sits in the chair closest to her, her fist curled over her thigh. "Darkwood insisted on opening Dark Falls to students again. It's only a matter of time before more people die."

Thea's delicate nose wrinkles. "Theodore Darkwood stole a sacred amulet from me, which he used to build and control the dome that prevents the hollows from swallowing Dark Falls whole. Unicorns swore not to meddle in earth's affairs anymore, but this time, I'm inclined to help." She and Deveraux exchange a knowing glance. "I will give you whatever ingredients you need to expose his part in Beth's murder, and the assassination of the mortals back in the day."

Dad whips his head in Thea's direction. "Darkwood was involved in the mortal students' deaths?"

The unicorn smooths down the skirt of her dress. "Yes. The hollows escaped their tomb once before in this century, right after your time at the Academy, Robert. They can't be *grabbed* or *moved* when they aren't safely tucked inside a body. To contain the crisis, Darkwood and his allies used the students as plastic bags to hold the hollows. They returned the bodies to the Dark Falls' sanctum, killed the students to keep the hollows from replicating, and buried the evidence." She draws in a slow, heavy breath. "A crime the highest-ranking officers of your government rewarded by nominating him to head of Senate…"

I knew Darkwood had used the students to contain the hollows, but clearly, no one else did. The stunned silence in the room allows me to take the lead.

"What's stopping him from using more innocent people to clean out the grounds?" I ask.

"He might be planning to, but he covets the treasure inside the crater, the source of Dark Falls' power. Hollows guard the entrance to the inner sanctum. That's why he stole the amulet from me. He thought it would make him impervious to them, but it only strengthened his forcefields."

Dad licks his lips. "This sacred amulet...is it made from a unicorn horn?"

Thea nods.

Barron squints at Thea, the shadows around him thicker by the second. "What's the source of Dark Falls' power?"

Of course, a pirate would only be interested in treasure.

Thea's lips twitch with barely-contained amusement. "A treasure meant for someone else than you, blakkr rauða."

My ears perk up. Whatever Barron is, Thea knows, and while I probably couldn't spell the words she just used, I make a mental note of them.

Barron squares his shoulders. "Can you help my friend get rid of her curse?"

Mallory hugs her arms to her chest. "I told you, Kay. Let it go."

Thea gives Barron a sad smile. "A curse can only be unwritten by its authors."

A green sheen spreads over Mal's face, and she squeezes her eyes shut, shaking her head.

Dad clears his throat. "I didn't think I'd ever see you again, Kayde."

"You and me both, Robert."

I squint at them. Barron let it slip that he knew *of* my dad, but I didn't think he knew him personally.

"You helped my daughters, despite everything..."

Barron's lips quirk. "They didn't give me much of a choice."

Dad sips on his tea. "And you...Your father was Mallon Chakrabarti." The soft tremble of his voice quickens my heart.

Mal's face pales in response, but she nods. "Yes, but my mother was a fury. A mortal."

I don't know much about the Underworld, but I know that surname. Malifar Chakrabarti was the name of the emperor that betrayed the peace between the three realms and started a war that ultimately destroyed his people.

"Now it all makes sense." Dad turns to Barron. "She's the reason you defected."

Barron balls his fists, and his shadows thrash around him. "Orders shouldn't always be followed. Especially when some shithead President sends you to kill an innocent little girl."

Dad's eyes dim, his gaze glued to Mallory. "After your mother's clan was slayed, you were branded with that curse to hide and weaken your powers—and also prevent the Chakrabarti sympathizers from kidnapping you and raising you off-world."

There's an eerie pause before Barron snarls. "You did it."

"Yes."

My eyes bulge. "Why?"

Mallory is frozen in place, her jaw slightly ajar, her eyes full of unshed tears.

"The President wanted to erase the Chakrabarti bloodline, but I thought if I cursed you, if I neutralized the immediate threat, then the High Council would leave you alone," Dad says.

Barron grips the armrest of his chair, shaking. "Well they didn't. They sent me after her anyway. She suffered for *decades* because of that curse."

"That was my mistake. A mistake I can finally rectify, if you'll let me." He offers Mallory his hand, speaking softly and with such care that I frown.

"I remember you..." Mal squints as though she's only now seeing him clearly, fury visible in her glacial-blue eyes. "How did you know my mother?"

In the pinch of my father's lips and the shameful hunch of his spine, I realize Mallory's mother wasn't just a woman Dad happened to cross paths with during his undercover mission.

In fact, I'm 99.9% positive Mallory's mother is Jules' mother.

15

EFFIGIES

Jules

The Faerie lodge where Cole and I spent our honeymoon is unrecognizable. Flynn guides me from the dusty portal to the balcony. Wilted flowers float on top of the basin where we used to swim. Wild vines grew over the banisters and nestled in the mortar between the stones.

Next to emerald water, a patch of grass was replaced by a marble statue depicting a round, fiery orb. My legs soften as we draw closer. Flames pierce the confines of my skin and reflect off the orb's silver plaque.

Fire that's closest kept burns most of all.

The engraved metal is cold under my fingers, and my belly squeezes painfully. "It's a grave."

"There was a body," Flynn says quietly—so quiet in fact, that I barely hear him. "We buried you, Jules. Right here."

Tears mist in my already red eyes. The foot of the tombstone is engraved with my name. My fingers tremble over the letters. "How—"

"If there hadn't been a body, we never would have stopped looking for you. Never."

Darkwood not only faked my death, he faked my *body*? He forced my dad, my friends, my husband to *bury* me?

Infernal magic pulses in my bones.

I hurl an orb at the tombstone, smashing the top half to pieces.

Flynn raises a brow.

"It's therapeutic," I say.

"Here, let me try it." He kicks the bottom with all his strength, and what's left of the headstone topples over.

Marble pieces pepper the ground after we're done.

I sit down in the grass to catch my breath. "Who's in that grave?"

"Beats me, but it wasn't a cheap spell or trick. It was you, down to the last beauty mark. It even smelled like you. I held your lifeless hand, I—" He sits next to me. "When the living copy of you came...I so badly wanted it to be you. I wasn't careful. She—it—whatever—was Unseelie. Cole saw through the lie in minutes, but she almost gutted him."

A sickening shudder trembles down my spine. "She pretended to be me to get to Cole?"

Flynn buries both hands inside his thick jacket. "It was the worst kept secret at court that Cole's grief was messing with his mind. One look at you now, and I feel like an idiot for thinking she was you."

I rub his shoulder. "Don't blame yourself. You couldn't have known."

The warmth of his skin melts the chill of the night. "I should have known. It didn't have your spark, your passion, your fire." He tucks a loose curl behind my ear, his sadness thick between us, taking a life of its own.

"I lost him, Flynn. He's not the same. He's...darker. Did you guys fall out over the doppelgänger thing, or was there something more?" I ask, thinking Cole could hardly hold that against Flynn for a decade.

His head hangs low between his shoulders. "It's not anyone's fault, really. We grieved differently. Cole threw his mind, body, and soul into the business of being King, and I did the opposite...we just couldn't find a way to *function* with you gone."

"What's *the opposite* of being king?" I ask.

His gaze falls to his lap. "I abused the bottle, and meaningless sex..."

"Imagine that." I ignore the sting in my chest and force a small smile on my lips, not wanting Flynn to feel ashamed for telling me the truth.

A quick chuckle lights his face, but he sobers up quickly. "Don't tease. Things got pretty dark for a while."

I wrap him up in my arms and place an apologetic kiss on his cheek. "I'm sorry."

He leans into my embrace. "Who knows, maybe his soul can heal now that you're back."

I swallow hard. "Did Cole remarry?"

Flynn shakes his head, and a hot sense of relief washes through me.

"What about Brie?" I breathe.

"If he had married Brie, he wouldn't have kept it a secret. The people have clamored for a queen since he became king. If you're asking if they're together...it's not the kind of thing I'd know anymore."

"And where is Erron?" I ask.

"Dead."

"Oh." My heart beats in my throat. Cole has lost his father and his uncle and Gods-know who else... "I guess we start in Dark Falls and figure the rest out from there."

Get back home. Expose Oz and Darkwood. Fix Dark Falls. Heal Cole. The list only adds up, more and more impossible tasks stacking on top of one another. The weight of it all threatens to floor me.

Flynn links our fingers. "You don't have to do it all yourself, you know?"

I stare at our joined hands.

For me, it's only been weeks since we slept together and I realized how deeply he cared for me. It doesn't seem like the time apart eroded his feelings but only made them stronger.

Salty tears mix on our tongues as we kiss. It's desperate and rash, full of regrets and fears.

"I love you, witch. I never got to say it," Flynn rasps, his blue gaze clear and wide. "I know you thought I only loved him—I certainly didn't want anyone to think—"

I press my index finger to his lips. "Shh."

"It's okay if you can't say it back. I've had years to mull it over. I stood over your fresh grave, I—"

"I love you, too." My throat dries up, but I find the courage to continue. "I love you even though you treated me horribly in the beginning, even though I love Cole, and I'm still at war with myself over the whole thing."

A sad smile glazes his lips. "Most earthlings think loving more than one person at a time is impossible."

"I'm not one of them."

He presses his mouth to mine, softly. "Thank the gods for that."

I've pondered the question over the last few weeks, deep in the galley of the boat. I've asked myself how, as I'm without a doubt head over heels for Cole, I'm still drawn to Flynn so much. How being with the two of them had eroded the notion that to love someone, I had to withhold my love for all others.

With trembling fingers, I play with his silky hair and trace the nape of his neck.

I expect to feel some type of guilt, kissing, just the two of us, but it feels...right. His love is palpable in every brush, every nibble, and every lick. I pull him closer, eager to feel his warmth.

Flynn wrenches my thick sweater past my head, and my long, purple and red curls fall haphazardly around my face. "Fuck... you don't even look human anymore."

"What do I look like?" I tease him, one brow arched in question, wondering how his beautifully wicked mind works.

"A Goddess."

A moan escapes him when I stroke his hair, the golden locks deliciously tousled. His angelic aura eclipses the scenery and all the tangled emotions that came with it, my eyes solely focused on the unbridled joy lighting his face.

He dives in for a kiss, his hands shaking. "I still can't believe you're here."

Our tongues battle for dominance as he slides my pants off, leaving only my bra on, the clear need to be reunited in flesh taking precedence.

My stomach flips in need as I peel his pants down his ass, eager to see how badly he wants me. My impatience is only rivaled by his, our mouths fused and eyes closed, the urgency taking a life of its own.

Flynn envelops me like a wave, crashing hard and deep inside me in one long thrust, and gives me a few seconds to get used to him. "Fuck, I missed you."

I rake my nails along his back, and he bites my neck as though it could summon Cole back to us.

We move languidly, craving each other's touch beyond reason, chasing the friction of skin against skin, the movements slow and disarming. I glide my feet down his calves as he strokes the valley between my breasts, thrusting inside me with a mix of passion and muted reverence.

It's a plea, a prayer, and a chant.

A release of tension.

A beautifully desperate embrace, both of us hungry for the chaos of our lives to still for an instant, chasing a solace we can only find together.

16

ODDLY TRANSPARENT
FRIENDSHIPS

Jules

Flynn guides me through Faerie to the portal that leads back to Dark Falls, and we emerge near the force field that sent me flying through the air when Allie and I first returned from the Underworld. It's midday here, and the sun is high in the sky. The ruins of the dining hall are silent, no hollows visible within its walls.

"A few hollows are stuck inside what's left of the building, but the spell holding them in there is shaky at best. Let's hurry." Flynn marches over to the force field and uses his magic to carve a dimensional ring the size of a door into it. Flynn was never one to be bothered by closed doors and impregnable walls. I'm in awe of his talent—and totally jealous.

On the other side of the foggy barrier, the Dark Falls library's exterior is exactly as I remember it. Stone gargoyles lounge in the sun on the staircase's banisters, their eyes closed.

Flynn barrels past them and holds the door open for me.

The chandelier twinkles above our heads.

"Jules!" Lydia jumps to her feet a few desks down in a series of cubicles. A long red braid cascades over her shoulder, but she hasn't aged a day.

"Lydia." I skip over to my best friend and pull her into a warm embrace, which she reciprocates tenfold.

"Oh gods, I missed you so much." She squeezes me tight.

A hint of sadness pierces my excitement. "I'm so happy to see you. Where's Allie? Did she come through here?"

Lydia releases me. "Yes. She went with Rose Deveraux to get help."

Flynn smiles at my side. "Nice to see you too, Red."

"Hey, Flynn." She throws her arms around him in greeting.

I gape.

My best-friend and the guy that used to terrify her beyond reason hug like they're old friends, and once again I tremble at the consequences of my trip to the Underworld. Everything is different, and while this is *good-different*, it still unnerves me.

Flynn keeps one arm around her shoulders and brings me inside the huddle. "How's my chess piece going, any progress?"

A chuckle warms Lydia's answer. "Yes, I finished it."

Flynn skips over to the huge chess board on one of the desks and snatches a black piece from the board. His lop-sided grin melts into a puppy-dog pout. "He looks...drunk."

Lydia's shoulders hitch. "It's supposed to be realistic."

I grab the arch of my brow. "Oh wow. I'm totally freaked out that the whole world changed while I was puking my entrails out on a boat for only three weeks, but *this*—" I motion between the two of them— "I need more of *this*." I turn to Lydia. "You could barely speak in his presence before, what happened?"

Flynn inventories the chess pieces. "Red and I got shit-faced a bunch of times to honor your memory."

Lydia gives him the stink eye. "I don't know if I'd frame it like that."

The Fae drags his feet to us. "She just got back."

"We should be transparent with her," Lydia growls.

I squint at them in turn, a current of awkwardness suddenly rolling off of them. "Transparent about what?"

"We had sex. It was before I found out you were alive," Lydia blurts out, a vicious blush coloring her cheeks.

Flynn's eyes widen like he's been caught with his hand in the cookie-jar—or in this case, up my best friend's skirt. "I only went down on you."

"It counts," Lydia clips.

Flynn huffs. "It does *not*."

"Guys, guys, relax. I'm not—I mean, it's okay." A tiny ember of jealousy flickers in my chest, but the obvious guilt burning through Lydia snuffs it out immediately. I have no obvious stake on Flynn, and I had no expectation that he remained celibate for years, as he already admitted that he slept with a bunch of people while I was *dead*. I'm relieved to hear they're not a couple—that might have been weird— but I have no desire for them to feel bad.

My brain spirals down the rabbit hole, and I grip Lydia's hand. "We need to talk." I pull her toward the stairs.

Flynn inches forward. "Can I come?"

"No," we answer in unison.

I guide Lydia to the basement, to the restricted section, where we spent so many hours studying. This part of the library hasn't changed a bit, and a heavy sense of nostalgia grips me. Fire reflects off the stone walls, and the familiar scent of mildew tugs at my heart.

"Are you mad?" Lydia asks.

I shake my head, instinctively heading for my usual table. "I have feelings for Flynn, but everything is so fucked up, I'm absolutely *not* mad at you."

"That's a relief."

I glance at her from the corner of my eye. "How did you know I was alive? And are you working in Dark Falls now?"

"I had this recurring dream after I started painting the first piece of my chessboard set. I realized after a few weeks I was dreaming about the *future*, and you were part of it. I told Flynn, of course, but after what happened with the Unseelie... I don't think he could bear to get his hopes up."

I sink into my usual seat. "It explains how quickly he accepted my return."

"As for working here... Rose and I volunteered to tend to the force fields and gardens. We took over Summer Hall, and we tolerate Darkwood's oversight because it allows us to keep an eye on him." Lydia slips a few volumes from Beth's stack and piles them up on the desk. "Elsbeth's personal collection mentioned the origins of magic, and the center of Dark Falls' power. The hollows are a plague, of course, but they're not the worst of it. After the big earthquake, an underworld portal stretched under the school, a horizontal tear that swallows the ground inch by inch."

"How big are we talking?"

She opens one volume to a hand-drawn map of the academy. "Can you feel the tremble of magic under our feet? It runs under the whole school. We have managed to contain it so far, but the next earthquake might swallow what's left of Dark Falls and trap the whole state inside the timesink."

A shiver quakes my body. "That's...too big."

She hugs another book to her chest. "Come with me. I have to show you something else."

We pick up Flynn upstairs and Lydia guides us to the edge of the unending forest. We hike through the autumn leaves to the entrance of the cave Beth showed me before she died—so close to the Underworld tear that changed the course of my life forever.

A geodesic dome protects the area with a special force field, a thick, opaque bronze-gold wall that emits ten times the power of the others.

Hands on her hips, Lydia stares down the semi-transparent surface of the dome. "Whatever you have to do, it starts here. This barrier holds in the balance of the 40-something hollows that haven't yet breached the perimeter. The other force fields are meant to control the few that got away.

"There's something down there, at the heart of Dark Falls. Something that could save or destroy us." Her green gaze bores into me. "And I'm certain we shouldn't let Darkwood find it."

She's right. My instincts scream that whatever is beyond that dome is powerful enough to rewrite history, and we can't let Theodore Darkwood anywhere near it.

"How do we get past the dome?" The energy from the thick wall prickles my fingertips.

Flynn raises a hand to the barrier, and his arm shakes. A bead of sweat glides down his forehead. "It's impervious to my powers."

"It's not a typical Magisterium enchantment. Its magic signature is different, similar to the spell Elsbeth used to keep Summer Hall warm. The only one that can penetrate it is Darkwood. He controls it with an eight-point star talisman he wears around his neck." Lydia shows us a picture of the amulet.

Beth's meticulous calligraphy fills in the margins.

"It's an amulet made from a unicorn horn," I breathe.

Flynn runs his hand over the surface of the dome again. "How do we steal it from him?"

"I'm not sure. The inauguration of the new building is in a few days. Darkwood almost never comes to Dark Falls anymore, because of the timesink, but he'll come for this. Magisterium security will be in full swing."

I pull my brows together. "Do we really want to move on Dark-wood during such a public event?"

Lydia stares down the dome with both hands on her hips. "Allie and Rose went to the unicorns for help. With a bit of luck, it won't be long before they return, and we can hatch a plan."

"The unicorns?" A heavy sense of doom hovers in my chest. "There's still so much I need to know."

"Let's go back to the library, and I'll tell you all about it," Lydia offers with a smile.

Flynn squeezes my shoulder. "Let's go. I'm famished."

17

WAKE ME UP

Jules

The underbelly of the library possesses the most mystical quality. Here, in the restricted section, books are alive. They buzz with memory, their spines allowing for a current of secrets to pass through the aisles. I'm sitting in a lotus position at the foot of Beth's personal stack when the air electrifies with power.

Contrary to the irregular pulses quaking Dark Falls, this power is seductive. Insidious. And frighteningly comforting.

I feel him before he appears. All the hairs on my arms rise as I look up from the parchment and meet Cole's burning, incensed gaze.

His silhouette obscures the light of the torches, his shadow looming between the two stacks. "I should have chained you to my bed."

The raspy admonishment glides along my skin like thick Fae water. Suffocating and yet...enticing, and I'm reminded of all the other petty fights we had in here, arguing amongst the dusty collection. We resisted the pull between us with every fiber of our beings, and yet, we always ended up here, whispering in candlelight. The familiarity of it all steals my breath, and I half-expect Pembrooke to fly in to shush us, but we're alone.

"Then do it." I snap my book shut and flash Cole a mischievous smile, summoning the sassy part of me, the girl I was only months ago that didn't carry so much weight on her shoulders.

There's no way Flynn and Lydia didn't feel Cole's arrival, but I'm grateful for the chance to talk to him alone.

"You're coming back to Faerie with me *now*."

I spring to my feet and turn my back to him, skipping over to the table we used to share. "Don't tell me what to do."

He chases after me…as I knew he would. "You will do as I tell you. I'm your *King*."

"Are you supposed to be here? Isn't it dangerous? Last I heard, you were wanted for murder." I hop on the table and face him, legs dangling from the edge.

We spent countless hours here, and the torches cast familiar shadows on the walls. A black wool sweater licks the network of silvery scars that descends to his collarbone, but other than that, he's my wicked Fae prince, and I'm as impulsive and determined as ever.

He prowls forward. "Being King has its perks—diplomatic immunity being one of them."

The decade between us is invisible to the naked eye. Here, in a realm that tempers his other-worldly shine, he's not a grumpy, all-powerful monarch.

He's all mine.

His gaze travels from the knotted blouse tied above my belly button to my colorful curls. "It's not a game."

"It never was." I link my arms around his neck, and he allows it.

He could zap us back to Faerie in an instant, to his Hall of Mirrors, without my consent, but I'm banking on his curiosity to subdue the primeval part of him that clearly means to drag me back to his chambers by the hair.

He presses his forehead to mine as my legs make space for him, my thighs snug against his sides. The magnetic pull between us takes a life of its own in the secluded, secret part of the library where we spent so many hours studying, observing each other, breathing *together*. The fruity aromas of his skin soften my knees, yet, a sense of anguish still separates us.

I skim the soft fabric of his shirt. "Are you in love with somebody else?" The fear drives me nuts, dark and heavy, and I can no longer reign it in. "I saw Brie at the palace…"

"Brie saved the realm. I owe her everything…" Regrets drip from his tongue. There's real love in his answer, his devotion to her muted, but present all the same.

Jealousy sinks its nasty nails in my heart, along with a heavy sense of acceptance. If he moved on, if he made promises to her… To hell with it. He was mine first.

"—but I could never give her what she really wanted."

I breathe a little easier. "No?"

"After my father died, she dealt with my siblings' doubts and convinced them I was fit to be King. She took care of me, tolerated my mood swings, my grief…but despite my best efforts, I couldn't let her in. She stayed by my side regardless and handled the palace's servants, the parties, and the overall bustle of court." He grazes the side of my face, his fingers tangled in my rebellious curls. "I'm not the boy you married."

I run my fingertips down his wrist to his elbow, my chest tight with the promise of his kiss. "You are."

Eyes cast down, he shakes his head. "I work day and night, but the Unseelie still win battles, and unrest grows in the territories. On top of it all, I'm itching to ram my fist through Darkwood even though it'd mean war with Earth. Since I became King, I've had no time to *breathe*."

Our gazes meet, and he doesn't look away.

"I love you."

"You called me a *monster*."

Fuck, no water under that bridge.

The instinct to defend myself rears its head. "You casted an irreversible spell on me without my consent, and it came with this huge weight. I needed time to process."

"When Erron told me about the ritual, I couldn't get it out of my head. I knew releasing Beth's spirit was important to you, and it had to be done on an unsuspecting soul, so it made sense." Our lips brush. "But mostly, I was scared shitless of losing you."

I grip his hand and press it to my beating heart. "I'm here. You have me."

"I should have looked for you. I can't forgive myself for being duped by Darkwood, for abandoning you—" he frees himself from my grasp, eyes cast down. "If I hadn't been so stubborn, I would have been with you that night, and none of this would have happened."

I try to meet his gaze. "I was angry, too. I pushed you away."

He shakes his head. "You were right. I shouldn't have done it without your consent, or at least tried to find a better way to do it."

"Thank you. It means a lot, even if years have technically gone by, it's still…raw for me."

"I'm sorry."

I cup the side of his face. "I forgive you."

"All these years lost…because of *me*," he whispers.

Our noses bump as I lean in. "We're together *now*. Nothing else matters."

The pad of his thumb travels across my cheekbone to my bottom lip. The move is slow and methodical, and it feels like it's part of some sacred, ancient ritual meant to worship me—before cutting me to pieces.

Cole swallows my hungry moan with his lips, his tongue impatient as his hand continues its journey past my chin to the hollow of my neck. We kiss as though we're holding our last breath, eager to rediscover each other. I let the bright, unwavering need swallow everything else.

He spreads my blouse open, one button at a time, and untangles the knot in my shirt. Cold air blows across my chest, and my entire body tingles in anticipation.

I reach under his shirt and drag it up his chest, dying to feel his heat. He curls a hand around mine, stopping my ascension, but not before I feel the deep imprint of a scar on his left pectoral muscle.

Our gazes meet again.

Lips pressed in a thin line, Cole allows me to work the shirt over his head, revealing the deep, iridescent scars. Deep claw marks dig into the left side of his chest, like the monster almost ripped his heart out. Fire rages to the surface of my skin. I want to burn the world down to find this creature and bring it pain.

The fire slips beyond my control and burns through my clothes.

"Did you kill whatever did this to you?" I ask through clenched teeth.

"Not yet."

"We'll do it together." I reign in the urge to pity my warrior king, knowing his pride will not stand it.

"The mark is nothing." He digs his nails into the scar. "I'm dead... on the inside."

I rest a hand over his wild heart. "You're obviously not."

Our noses touch, his breath hot on my lips. "Bring me to life, Fire Girl."

He dusts off fiery embers from my shoulders and swallows my answer with a kiss. I fight his tongue for dominance as he drags my pants and underwear off in one fluid motion.

I tug on his belt, working the buckle open, delighted to find out he's not wearing anything underneath his pants. A purr escapes me when I push his clothes out of the way and wrap my hand around his hard length, stroking it up and down.

He curls his hands into fists, clearly holding himself back.

I happily take the lead, guide Cole to the rug and climb over him. The carpet chafes my knees as I discard my blouse.

He clings to me, hands in my hair, as though I'm the last thing tethering him to this realm, and kisses me stupid before sliding his hands down to knead my breasts.

I arch my back, delirious, my core so wet I can barely think, aching for his fullness to stretch me to the limit between pleasure and pain.

His jaw clenches as I align myself with his throbbing cock, taking it in inch by inch.

I rock back and forth, and Cole teases and pinches my nipples until I writhe on top of him.

"You're still holding back," I whisper, heady with lust, my orgasm already banging at the door.

"I don't want to *make love* to you. I want to *consume* you…" He grips my hips, pushing deeper inside me, so deep it almost hurts.

A small cry escapes me.

Cole sucks my nipple inside his mouth, sending me over the edge. I quake in his arms, the throb between my legs greedy for more, my thirst for him unquenched.

He rolls on top of me, pining me beneath him, and traces a fiery path between my breasts. "I've dreamt about you so many times… couldn't even set foot in Dark Falls after you disappeared."

I trace the curve of his mouth. "I'm here. You won't break me."

"I'm not who I used to be."

"I don't expect you to be."

I need to make peace with the time I lost.

He thrusts inside me again, this time without hesitation. I scrape my nails across his back and eagerly drink the sorrows off his lips. We move in sync, both chasing the friction between our bodies with passion and fury, desperate to feel whole again.

Cole snaps his hips *just so*, and I whimper. "Don't stop."

He drags himself out all the way before crashing inside me again. I run my fingers along the ridges in his back, my walls clenching forcefully around him as he rides out my second orgasm.

I'm a junkie when it comes to him, his touch my special brand of euphoria.

Goosebumps freckle his neck, and the muscles in his shoulders coil before he picks up the pace, teetering on the edge.

He's so beautiful in this moment, naked, hungry, and so undoubtedly mine.

I lean into his ear. "Come for your queen."

He grips my hands and holds them above my head, the quick and perfect response riling me up, and my knuckles sink into the carpet at my back.

An insolent grin twists his mouth. "Only if you scream my name."

Cole sinks inside me over and over again with a precise, calculated pace that mollifies my bones. He fucks me slow and steady until I can't tell where he ends and I begin, my breath hot in his ear.

"Please...I need more."

He glides one hand between us and rubs the sensitive bundle of nerves between my legs. I arch my back off the ground and give him exactly what he wants, falling apart in his arms again, his name echoing along the stone walls.

He holds me flush against him, his mouth on my throat. "Louder."

Boy, do I want to scream *for* him.

With him.

Forever.

We catch our breaths, entangled in each other. The scent we made together lulls me into a dream-like state.

Cole reaches above our heads to pick up the book I was reading when he arrived and leafs through it. "Are you researching a particular spell to knock Darkwood off his pedestal?"

"Lydia wanted me to read this book—Beth wrote it herself, and according to her, it relates to the origins of the hollows and how to stop them. She said she's been dreaming about it a lot."

He wets his lips and begins to read the marked page out loud. "A legend amongst legends, the Phoenix sang one last melody before it died, and parted with pieces of itself so the love it had found in the mortal world would survive."

My knees soften at the low pitch of his velvety voice, and I curl into him.

"One drop of its blood transformed a mortal into a vampire.

A gold scale gave another a mermaid tail.

Pieces of its beak broke off and created hybrids; griffins and chimera.

Its feathers could rearrange bones, and it let his closest friends pluck his tail. Shifters were born.

Before it flew into eternity, it looked at the mortals left and cried, for it had nothing else to give them.

Its tears splashed over them, giving them control over the elements."

I place a loving kiss on my husband's shoulder, thrilled to be able to touch him again. "It's beautiful, but I don't see how it relates to us or the hollows."

"I don't either." He caresses my hair.

Eyes half-mast, I ask, "What happened with Flynn? He told me you guys fell out."

Cole squares his shoulders. "He drank himself to the brink, and I didn't know how to deal with him anymore, so I sent him away."

"To guard Dark Falls?"

He nods. "The time difference made it easy to avoid him."

"You should talk to him."

He waves my concerns away. "Maybe later..after all this."

His non-committal response creates an empty space in my belly, and I'm about to argue when Lydia's voice echoes through the stacks. "Hey, guys. I don't want to intrude, but it's really time to get dressed now."

I glance at her over the books. She's holding one hand in front of her eyes, and I can't help but giggle at the sight, my heart so full of joy it might burst. I'm back in Dark Falls, and even though *everything* is messed up, I've got my infuriating husband, my best friend, Flynn...

"Allie's back. Your father is with her, and he's really antsy to see you, so..."

My eyes widen, and I pat my messy hair, well aware that I look, for lack of a better word, freshly fucked. Cole quickly slips on his pants, clearly not thrilled by the idea of my father finding us naked.

I clutch my blouse in a hurry and button it back up. "Hold on. We're coming."

"I think you've already come," Cole says wickedly.

I slap his arm. "Shut up."

"Three times."

A nervous giggle pops out of my throat. Men.

18

GREEN TAILS

Jules

Tension is palpable on the library's first floor. Clouds obscure the moon, the glow of the chandelier warm and inviting compared to the forest outside. Trent chats with Flynn and Lydia at her desk, apparently chummy with them now.

Brie sits a few feet behind them, in all her pissed-off mermaid glory, arms crossed over her chest. Her clothes and Cole's are color-coordinated, and my stomach clenches. I guess Cole, Trent, and Brie somehow traveled in from Faerie together.

Silence washes over the room as we draw near.

Mallory stands up from the bench she shared with Barron. "Hi."

"Mal…You're a girl again," I say.

"I am." She bites her bottom lip, a dark frown on her face. "It's a long story."

Did she break the curse? Were the unicorns able to help as Beth did with me?

Dad rushes over from the stacks, leaving Deveraux and Allie to their conversation. "Munchkin!"

"Dad." I skip over to my father, ignoring the tense looks between him and Cole as my dad hugs me like he never expected to see me again.

Cole leans against the closest stack, withdrawn from the group.

"How long has it been for you?" I ask, the question quickly becoming a fucked-up version of, "what did you do this weekend?"

"Too long, Munchkin. Way too long." One last tight squeeze empties my lungs before he lets me go and straightens his old-fashioned jacket.

Allie waves me over to her. With a sheepish smile, I point discreetly at Cole and join him instead. She glowers at my husband, her lips curled down, but I'll make it up ot her later. Right now, I need to stand by my husband.

Deveraux clears her throat. "Julia, I'm glad to see you. And Cole…" Her eyes flash, not in warning, exactly, but an understanding passes between them. "It's not every day the Fae King visits Dark Falls."

"I'll be more open to your invitations in the future." Cole caresses my spine and throws a lazy arm around my neck, holding me to him. The simple, easy gesture melts my insides, and Flynn throws me a discrete thumbs up.

A huge grin threatens to overpower my face, but I force my attention back to Deveraux.

The professor meets the eyes of every single person in the room in turn. "Darkwood made one humongous mistake. He used Julia and Allie's 'deaths' to build a case for his dictatorship. Two young, powerful witches had perished in the earthquake, eaten alive by hollows…it was a powerful image."

Allie's jaw drops. "He used us to gain power?"

"He used Robert's guilt and grief as a stepping stone, highlighting how the elemental party had done too poor a job to protect the school and couldn't possibly protect the realm. He twisted the story to fit his needs. You, Allie, were painted as a princess that perished too soon, and Julia..." Her gaze collides with mine, a hint of regret thick in her voice.

Trent scoffs. "He used Jules as the poster child against Faerie's involvement in our affairs, convincing everyone she'd been used and discarded by their new King."

Dad's fists clench at his sides, and the bitter curl of Brie's mouth speaks volumes.

Lydia squeezes Trent's shoulder. "And he bargained his own son away."

After Trent visited us in Cole's war tent, I never got the full story detailing how the vampire had ended up in Faerie, but judging by Lydia's angry pout, Theodore really fucked things up with his son.

"How does that help us?" I ask, thinking Deveraux must already have a plan.

A small smile tugs at the corners of her mouth. "Dark Falls' new building will be inaugurated in a few days. Darkwood will be there, along with the entire High Council, and all the major players in government. Some of them are too corrupt, eating out of the palm of his hand, but others could rally to our side. If we reveal that you girls are alive, and what really happened the day of the earthquake, it should damage his reputation beyond repair."

"Your very survival might be enough to shatter him, so if he gets a chance to kill you and bury you quietly, he'll take it," Trent adds, looking straight at me.

Lydia raises her hand to speak. "Won't everyone think they're just good copies, like the ones we buried?"

"Their true identity will be called into question, that's for sure, but could easily be proven," Deveraux answers.

Brie snickers, "If Darkwood doesn't arrest us first."

A bubble of nerves hovers in my chest. It'll be hard, but together, we might actually have a shot at taking down Darkwood. "We need enough time to make our case and expose his lies, so he can't spin this in his favor, too."

"Yes, we need a captive audience," Lydia says.

Deveraux dumps a large leather book on the desk with a loud

thump. "I have an idea. Amalthea gave us some prized ingredients. I will brew a petrifying spell that can be activated at the desired time. We will spike everyone's drinks and make sure they are not only able to hear what we have to say, but forced to do so."

Dad uncrosses his arms with a solemn nod. "As unlawful as it sounds, I've exhausted all the legal channels. I say it's time to fight fire with fire."

"Any Magus worth its salt will have an array of basic antidotes at his disposal. Petrifying spells need a minute to settle in, and to affect a crowd of this size, we'll have to spread out in the room and cast the spell at the exact same time. They're bound to notice," Lydia says.

Brie smiles wickedly. "Unless we create a distraction big enough to hold their attention."

Lydia raises her index finger to the mermaid. "We're not setting fire to the forest again."

Barron finally joins in the conversation, his voice full of barely-contained power. "I have something below deck that could help." His gaze latches on to Allie. "A dress that will ensure everyone at the party looks only at you, little storm. What do you say?"

Allie bites her bottom lip. "Alright."

"I'm invited, so I can bring a plus one. Allie can come with me," Flynn says.

"And we're invited, too," Brie announces, the *we* she's referring to making me want to punch her smug face. "Though I think no one expects Cole to show up."

Deveraux leafs through the big grimoire. "The soirée is a masquerade ball. Julia and Lydia will mix in with the staff, unnoticed. Robert, Cole, Brie, Flynn, Trent, Allie, and I can attend as guests."

Lydia bites her thumb. "But how are we going to get in with the staff?"

Trent rises to his feet. "Leave that to me."

That puts everyone besides Barron in the ballroom, and as happy as I'd be to bring Theodore Darkwood's reign to an end, I fear we're all forgetting something.

"Let's not forget about Oz. He needs to be dealt with, too."

Blood drains from Allie's face.

"Osbourne mostly did Darkwood's bidding. He's only liable if he knew the orders he received were unsanctioned by the Senate or High Council."

Allie's jaw ticks. "He knew."

Dad pats her shoulder. "I know, Peanut, but proving it will be hard, if not impossible."

Deveraux's quill scratches along a blank piece of parchment. "Let's cut off the roots at the rot. We can worry about the weeds later. I need all these ingredients for this spell," her eyes flick in my direction, "and Julia's help."

Dad clears his throat. "Infernal magic can't be the answer here."

Deveraux hands the list to Lydia. "We need *all* the magic, Robert. Julia, wait for me here. I have to get a grimoire from my bedroom."

I tilt my head in agreement.

Dad follows after her with Allie in tow, his footsteps a bit hurried like he still hopes to change Deveraux's mind about using infernal magic.

Barron flanks Lydia. "Let me help with some of these ingredients."

My best friend throws her black coat over her shoulders and motions him along.

Brie hangs back, her arms crossed tightly around her chest, hovering. She clearly wants to talk to Cole one-on-one.

He tucks his chin and releases me from his embrace. "Give me a minute."

I watch them head outside, my heart in knots. I suppose it's okay for Cole to have feelings for her, just as I love Flynn. My husband has his own history with the blond Fae, and it never bothered me before, but selfishly, I need him to love me *more*.

Flynn jumps out of his seat, a dark shroud obscuring his features. "The bastard couldn't even say hello." He barrels toward the stairs leading to the restricted section, mumbling unintelligible curses below his breath. "Do not follow me. I need a minute."

The thundercloud of power in his wake tells me this is not merely a suggestion. What the fuck happened between them while I was gone? *I sent him away* doesn't seem to cover the depth of Flynn's reaction.

That leaves Trent in the library with me, so I take Lydia's seat by him.

We exchange nervous glances.

"Why do you want to help us?" I ask the vampire, our history weighing on my mind.

"I ended up in Faerie because Kirkan demanded reparations for your death, in typical Fae style. He was entitled to it by some serpentine law, since you—a Fae princess—had died on my father's watch. Well, my father could have found a way around that law, or offered anything else, but he sold me out to his enemy."

"Why?" I'm struggling to fit all the pieces of the puzzle together, wondering what in the dark gods' name would have pushed Darkwood to get rid of his own son.

"He insisted that I should swear my life and obedience to the Fae King to spy on them and prevent a potential attack, but I quickly realized the Fae weren't conspiring against us. They were far too busy waging war on the Unseelie. In fact, my father only aimed to destroy their influence on the Council for his own personal gain. I want to take him down as much as you do."

I squeeze his lower arm, my heart breaking for him, but his words music to my ears. Somehow, in the decade that I missed, Trent and I ended up on the same side again, and the thought warms my heart.

"I'm sorry he treated you that way." I rest my hand over his for a split second. "And I'm glad we're on the same side again."

"Oh, I'm on your side," a warm smile stretches his lips, "but I still think Cole is an egotistical prick."

"Err—" I hesitate.

Despite the harsh words, mischief dances in his garnet eyes. "Seriously though, he could have made my life hell, but he didn't. I think in memory of you."

"It's so strange. For me it's only been weeks since I left Dark Falls."

He sobers up, his face a shade whiter than it was a minute ago. "I wasn't kidding, you know. My father would kill us all, if necessary. Whatever happens at the ball, you need to be careful."

"I promise."

Funny how only weeks ago, I sat with him downstairs in the library, certain we could never be on the same side again. That'll teach me to take anything in this life for granted.

"Winslow. A word?" Brie chucks out from the doorway, her face green.

I follow the mermaid to the middle of the stacks. Scales fade in and out on her arms as she paces the aisle. A salty mist freckles my face when she suddenly comes to a halt and plants a kiss on my lips.

I jerk away. "What are you doing?"

She cries out in frustration. "Isn't it my only play? The one chance I have to remain in his life? Flynn managed to worm his way inside your relationship—"

"Flynn is different. We care for each other. You don't even *like* me."

A foursome is out of the equation because Brie simply sets my teeth on edge.

"True. In fact, I hate you. How does it feel? To know the most powerful man in the three realms can't go to sleep without seeing your face? That he was so broken by your death that he almost burned down the world?"

"You're exaggerating—"

"I've loved him my whole life. Do you know how it feels to live for someone who doesn't love you back? To hold his hand when he's injured and clean up his messes while he grapples at every violent distraction he can find? To see him keep himself imprisoned in a well of grief so deep that you have no hope he'll ever make it out?"

I swallow the hard lump in my throat. Despite all the jealousy, and our differences, I'm grateful to her for taking care of Cole during his darkest days.

Brie's arms fall at her sides. "I hate you because losing you caused him so much *pain*."

"It wasn't my choice," I croak.

"I'm not saying it makes sense." With that, she buries her hands in her jacket and walks off. The salty aftertaste of her tears mist the air.

19

SCORNED WITCH

Allie

Cinderella's late for the ball. My promiscuous escort is not known for his punctuality, so I watch the first guests arrive from the comfort and security of a tall pine. The new dining hall is twice as big as the old one, with an indoor pool and a ballroom.

I couldn't care less about it, but I need to catch a glimpse of Daniel. I need a moment alone to see him, his new fiancée, and his treacherous smile.

My ex-lover steps out of the gates' portal flanked by his men, and I hold my breath. From afar, he hasn't changed a bit. A tailcoat white jacket with a matching undershirt molds his body, a fancy, old fashioned look I've never seen on him. His back is to me as he chats with the agents. I can almost hear what they're saying, but not quite.

The caterers and waiters—along with Lydia and Jules—are already inside the building. According to Deveraux, the Magisterium is mostly there to protect Darkwood and his guests from the hollows, not to swarth a political *coup d'état,* but their numbers unnerve me all the same. There's twice as many Magus as there were at Darkwood's inauguration ceremony, and I frown.

The black and gold Magisterium uniforms gleam in the night as his minions forge ahead to check the perimeter. Only a handful of them walk inside, the others head toward the force fields.

Daniel straightens the lapels of his jacket as Deveraux greets him out front, looking flawless in her gold-sequined pantsuit and matching heels. She answers his questions with an affable smile, and I wonder how she manages to stay so calm and collected, hiding her true allegiance, when I'm simply boiling inside.

She says something funny enough for Daniel to laugh, and the sound threatens to floor me. The closest pine needles dry up and fall, electrified by my powers, and I struggle to catch my breath.

Daniel Osbourne duped me, but his smile still steals my breath. How is that fair? I bite back bile and fly low between the trees, back to the library. I need to change and join the party—hopefully without choking on my damn tears.

Flynn chats with Trent on the steps outside the library when I get back.

"It's almost showtime, witch. You better change," the blond Fae says. His white blonde hair gleams with Faerie dust, slicked back over his head, the sides shorter than the top, a perfect mix between a heartthrob and a villain. A pair of black masks hangs from his loose grip.

"I know." I rush past the two men and stone gargoyles, my gut in knots. "Magisterium agents are already spreading across the grounds. We have to clear out of here."

A sheen of sweat sticks to my temples, so I rush to the bathroom, splash cold water on my face, and unbutton my blouse.

Barron prowls in behind me and closes the door. A black garment bag is wrapped around his lower arm, and hunger pulses in his gaze. The distance between us melts until I feel his heat, his thunderous aura raising all the hairs on my neck to attention. The memory of our kiss is enough to convince me that I can't afford a second round. Not tonight.

I press a decisive finger to his lips. "None of that. If I'm to survive the night, I can't let you steal my pain. I need it."

Without it, I fear my heart might crumble.

I snatch the dress from his grasp, hang it on a light fixture, and strip to my underwear.

He balls his fists and leans his forehead on the closest stall.

A genuine grin curves my lips. Serves him right for stripping in front of me the very first day we met. I can play games, too.

His dark aura thrashes, and his hands shake like he's dying to rip off the red lace of my underwear and drink my rage in until we cross a line that should never be crossed. "Yer fury drives me mad, little storm."

"Being attracted to scorned women is so…fucked up."

"Complicated, maybe." He grips my waist and pulls me flush against his chest. "But it's not like craving revenge is your only quality."

"You like women who occasionally yell at you?"

He shakes his head. "I like when *you* yell at me."

The heat emanating from him erodes my resolve, and my lids flutter. The smokey scent of incense and aftershave washes over me. How I wish I could get rid of my pain in this thunderous man's embrace. He holds me to him with care, and my rotten heart gives a big thump.

"I need to change." I escape his grasp, unzip the bag and slip the smooth, fresh fabric over my head.

The black silk shimmers with rainbow patterns.

"Move through the ballroom slowly, and be careful. Once you start to dance, the spell will activate. Its effect should only last a few minutes on experienced sorcerers."

I watch myself in the mirror. The dress is elegant and beautiful. The skirt almost touches the floor, and my back is left bare, but it's just a dress. I wonder what kind of magic Barron used to imbue it.

"What if they're human?" I ask.

He caresses my bare back, sparking goosebumps along my neck.

"They would spend the entire night in awe of you, frozen in contemplation."

"Is that what you do for a living? Smuggle forbidden artifacts?"

"Is there a more fascinating line of work than to explore the blurry, delicious lines between rage and beauty? Revenge and hope?" His hand slips down the small of my back to graze my ass.

I lean into his touch. "Careful. I wouldn't want to waste the dress."

A heavy breath skims my shoulder. He drinks in the curves of my body, his tattoos black enough to swallow the surrounding light. "Go and give them hell. When you return, I'll fuck you so hard and deep you won't remember that fucker's name."

I grip the sink with both hands, about ready to strip again and let him have me now. Gods.

Before I egg Barron on and dare him to take me in the bathroom, the door behind him opens.

With a knowing smirk, Flynn barrels ahead with no consideration for privacy and hands me one of the masquerade masks as though it's a corsage. He glances at Barron sideways. "Don't worry, Scary Dude, I'll keep close tabs on her."

"Not *too* close," Barron says through tight lips.

Flynn adjusts his own mask and checks himself out in the mirror. "Chill. I'm not interested."

"I know your type. You'd fuck anything on two legs."

A small laugh rumbles through the blond Fae. "True, but in this particular case, I have sufficient motivation not to." The cheery way he says the words nag me.

He's certainly not implying...

Not *Jules*?

I mean—he's had a wicked crush on her since the beginning, but she's with Cole. Why is he so fucking happy? I take his outstretched arm and follow him outside the library, still reeling from Barron's touch. Flynn's glamor picks at loose threads in my soul. I despise him, and yet my sister completely changed her mind about him. How?

I shake the unwanted hypothesis out of my brain. Who cares about Flynn Verinos?

Fate threw a drop-dead gorgeous vengeance guru in my path. Daniel was my first and only, but Barron will exorcize his memory from me, and I'm going to let him.

TWINKLE OF RED, purple, and yellow lights transform the new ballroom into a Mardi Gras fete. Feathers, sequins, and handcrafted masks hang on the walls, some of them enchanted to gaze back at us. The music is loud enough to muffle the conversations, a few dancers already busy in the center of the room. Tapas are being passed around by waiters wearing black livery and white masks, along with white hair pieces bursting with black feathers. I search for Jules or Lydia in the crowd.

Flynn leans in, his breath hot and heavy. "Cheer up. Our exes will totally freak out when they see us." He tucks the invitation back inside his red jacket's interior pocket and offers me his arm again.

I grind my teeth together. "They won't know who I am until it's too late. I'm wearing this stupid mask, remember?"

Flynn can be spotted a mile away, but I'm stuck in the role of the insignificant arm candy.

He guides me through the crowd, quite a few patrons stealing glances at him, whispering between themselves. "Still…picture their faces when you finally take it off. You get to fuck with your ex *and* the scary dude tonight. What else could be better?"

A man wearing all white brushes past us, stealing my breath, but a more thorough look confirms that it's not Daniel. I turn to Flynn. "You're speaking as though we've already won."

"Call it blind optimism. Ooh…Sushi." He snatches a maki from a tray and dumps it inside his mouth.

Anyone else would look unappealing or impolite cramming an oversized california roll inside his mouth, but Flynn dazzles me—and the whole room—with his glamor. He licks his thumb, and my insides curl at the urge to stand on my tiptoes and kiss him.

I growl. "Tone it down, already. Everyone's looking at us."

"Isn't that the whole point?"

"It's not time yet." I pull him deeper into the room and snatch a champagne flute from a tray. I need liquid courage, now more than ever.

Flynn stops me. "No alcohol, remember?"

Damn. I almost forgot Jules and Lydia were spiking everyone's drinks with Deveraux's spell. I discard the untouched flute discreetly, scour the room, and finally find Darkwood—and Daniel—on the other side of the dance floor. They chat near the buffet, a couple of Magisterium agents guarding the door behind them. Melanie looks gorgeous on Daniel's arm, her white dress and rose-gold mask flawless. I swallow hard. The goth chick I knew from school is certainly gone, and it enrages me how good they look together.

My mother joins Darkwood, wearing a similar fashion, and my jaw clenches.

She's alive and well, laughing with the girl that replaced *me*.

Electricity buzzes on top of my skin.

Flynn blocks my line of sight. "Easy. You need to chill, witch, or that dress—along with everyone here—will get fried." He points to the bar in the opposite corner of the room. "There's Jules."

The intimate way he slurs her name crawls under my skin. "I don't care how much time passed or what happened in Faerie. I won't let you use my sister."

"I love your sister."

"Err—" I grip the skirt of my dress and brace myself on his chest so I don't topple over.

He whisks me out to the outskirts of the dance floor, glowering. "*Careful* with the dress."

I lower my voice to a mere whisper. "Even if I believed you, she's not going to leave Cole for you."

"Who says she has to?"

Heat spreads on my cheeks at the loose wink he throws my way. Fae have never preached monogamy. I know that, yet his answer shocks me. It's uttered with more confidence than I expected.

"You guys have already slept together?"

He shrugs nonchalantly. "I don't kiss and tell."

I roll my eyes at the falsehood. "Ugh, please. How is that going to work?"

"We'll figure it out. Isn't that the whole point of relationships?"

"You'll always be the third wheel..." I trail off, still trying to grasp what the fuck happened in Faerie.

Flynn's forehead creases. "You're worried about my feelings?"

"No, I—" I slap his chest. "Shh—Melanie is coming this way."

He squeezes my hand in his. "Follow my lead, and whatever you do, do not speak to her." He pulls me to him and plants a long, devious kiss on my neck. I close my eyes, playing along, and emulate the look of wonder and pleasure I saw on many girls' faces when Flynn Verinos used his wicked tongue to arouse them.

Melanie slows down as she draws near, and Flynn releases me.

The vampire looks about to walk right past us before she crosses her arms. "Verinos, I see you're still obsessed with witches." She drags her eyes up and down my body, and her face crumples in question.

I bite my tongue not to reply, reacting as Flynn's date would, raising a brow at him, but the way Melanie stares at me sparks a flash of adrenaline in my blood. She's too close, and the mask only hides so much. We're screwed.

Flynn's radiant smile brings a blush to my cheeks. "Mel, I heard congratulations are in order. I can't believe that, after all these years, you're still fine with being second-best."

She flashes her canines, her interest in me gone. "What are you implying?"

"I heard Osbourne had his eyes set on a different political treasure..."

Mel growls. "Watch your filthy tongue."

I press my lips together not to grin. I know he's doing it to draw attention from me and rattle her to a point where her brain melts and she just wants to punch his face, but gods it feels good to see Melanie Darkwood squirm.

"Don't lie, Mel." Flynn's voice is low. Intimate. "You've always loved my tongue, along with the dirty, mind-blowing orgasms that came with it." He grazes her hip.

Almighty Melanie stutters. "I'm—I'm engaged. And you're with the barbie doll."

He throws me a loving smile before picking an imaginary lint off Melanie's dress. "She loves to watch. What do you say? We could visit the pool later..."

My cheeks heat up at the offer, and I wasn't even on the receiving end. I know it's a trick, a ploy to push Melanie off-balance and stroke Flynn's ego at the same time. Win-win.

But gods, she looks about to say yes.

Whispers and gasps buzz through the crowd, interrupting our conversation. All eyes turn to the front of the ballroom. Cole and Brie make their entrance, and even the most passionate dancers stop to stare.

Mel gapes, and Flynn wraps an arm around her shoulders. "You remember Cole, the King of Faerie?"

20

DEAD SWAN

Jules

*P*atrons hold their collective breaths as Cole and Brie waltz inside the ballroom, and my throat tightens. Cole's black jacket shimmers with gold, teal, and silver accents, matching the fabric of Brie's dress. It's infuriating that they look so damn good together.

I grit my teeth and return to my task.

The small white spheres containing Devereaux's spell dissolve into the wine instantly as they touch its surface, another tray of glasses ready for distribution.

My scalp itches because of the white wig, but Lydia and I blended in with the waitress crew without problems. Trent's surname certainly bought us a lot of leeway with the caterers.

Before I get started on the last batch of drinks, Oz walks over to the bar, barely two feet of space between us. "I'll have a martini, please."

I graze the edge of my mask, making sure it's still in place, and tuck the white spheres back inside my pockets, unwilling to take the chance that the dragon will figure out what I'm doing.

Shoulders stiff, I stare dead ahead not to cross his gaze and prepare his drinks.

He inches closer. "Hello, Julia."

With the most neutral expression I can muster, I wait, wondering if he's fishing, but as I meet his dangerous gray stare, I know I've been made.

A light chuckle colors his breath. "Dragons sense fire."

"You might have wings and scales, but you're no dragon—you're a snake," I hiss under my breath.

I can't cause a scene now, not when we're so close, so I concentrate on his martini instead.

"Nothing ever turned me on more than an honest woman. I'm thrilled to see you alive, really. Does this mean Allie—" he scours the room. "Ah, she's escorting the drunk Fae. Interesting. Care to let me in on your little plan?"

I grip the shaker. "Don't you dare look at my sister like that. You used angel dust to feel me up, you bastard."

"Did I? If I remember correctly, I didn't *order* you to kiss me. I asked if you found me attractive and if you *wanted* to kiss me. How was I to know you were lying? I merely *checked* that I hadn't misread your flushed ears and stuttered breaths—"

"You were dating my sister."

His shoulders hitch. "Like you don't know what it's like to crave two different men."

I hand him his drink, but I'd rather throw it in his face. "Don't pretend we're remotely similar."

"I admit...I didn't know you were alive." He dumps the glass on the table and grips the rim. "I don't like being played, so maybe you can tell me where you've been all these years, and why, and I won't alert Darkwood quite yet."

The deliberate distortion of a saxophone resonates around us, and Flynn whisks Allie to the dance floor.

A smirk festers on my lips.

Oz cranes his neck around to follow my gaze, but he can't stop us now.

I close my eyes not to be taken in by the spectacle created by Barron's enchanted dress. I'm already in position for the spell, and I peek at the corners of the room through my eyelashes. Lydia, Deveraux, Dad, Cole, and Brie, have all taken their spots.

Anyone who consumed even a drop of alcohol tonight will be petrified for a few minutes and forced to listen to what we have to say. We're either going to bring Darkwood down—or convince every dignitary here that we're terrorists.

Hell…we had to try something.

I murmur the incantation, and immediately, small gasps and shuddered breaths echo around the crowd. The band stops playing abruptly, either petrified, too, or shocked. Conversations, laughter, the clinking of glasses, and the ruffle of fabric give way to a perfectly frozen audience.

Flynn brings their dance to a halt. "Nicely done. We got their attention now," he says loud enough for everyone to hear.

The loud statement contrasts with the quiet, petrified guests. The Magus, Councilmen, and their dates—even Allie's mother—are all stuck in place.

Darkwood stirs, so he's not totally petrified, but gravely outnumbered. A snarl tears through his tight lips.

Cole prowls closer to him.

The old vampire's edges shimmer with rage. "You are as dangerous as I pegged you to be."

Cole stops a few feet from him, keeping a reasonable distance between them. "Just listen, Darkwood, and I won't have to kill you."

The clock is ticking.

Dad runs to Allie, and I double-check that Oz is affected by the spell before I join them in the middle of the room.

Dad clears his throat. "Dear friends and colleagues, I apologize for the unorthodox way we had to intervene tonight, but Theodore Darkwood made it impossible for me to talk to you through normal channels. In fact, I've waited a long time to finally speak the truth."

Allie and I peel off our masks, and I discard the wig to the ground.

"My daughters are alive. Darkwood fabricated their deaths, thinking they would never survive in the Underworld. He destroyed our political system and transformed the Magisterium into his personal army. Each of you knows this in your heart. He used our prejudice against the Fae, our fears of the hollows, to establish his dictatorship. Whenever we came close to restoring democracy, he fed into that fear to keep his power."

He pauses for a few seconds, his voice strong and unwavering, his resolve shining through his severe face. "In a minute, you will be released from this spell. Rose Deveraux and I will face the consequences of our methods, and we accept full responsibility for tonight, but Theodore Darkwood will not get out of this room without the truth being known by all. I call for a formal investigation on the President. To my knowledge, he ordered the death of Elsbeth Eillis, stole a priceless artifact from Amalthea herself, and left my daughters for dead in the underworld."

Cole strolls forward. "Theodore Darkwood has tried and failed to start a war with Faerie. I support Councilman Winslow in his search for the truth."

"And I," Brie declares solemnly at his side.

"And I." Trent walks out of the shadows. "Hey, Dad. Remember me?" He waves his hand in front of his father's face.

Golden sequins flash in the light as Deveraux marches to my dad, hands on her hips. "And I, as Dark Falls' head of faculty. I will release you now, and I promise none of us will try to flee."

The spell dissolves in an instant, and most of the petrified guests have to scramble to keep upright.

"Petty criminals...lying, probably under a Fae spell. Seize them," Darkwood seethes.

The agents present turn to their leader for a sign.

Oz gulps down the drink I prepared earlier in one swig before rubbing his chin. "Shouldn't we check the girls' identity first? Now that we are all gathered?"

What the hell is he playing at?

The crowd murmurs its assent.

A short-haired woman with emerald green hair walks forward. "I propose an immediate Swan trial. Councilman Winslow's accusations are of the gravest nature. Enough of us are here to stand witness. Let the truth speak for itself." By the chime of her hypnotic voice and her appearance, I figure she's Elsa Demers, the infamous Sea Queen.

I hold my breath. A swan trial is an extremely rare and potent way to establish the truth, but it's reserved for conflicts of apocalyptic proportions.

Darkwood spreads his arms. "I have nothing to hide." The snide curve of his mouth telegraphs only one thing: he thinks he's going to win.

The amulet he stole from the unicorns must also make him impervious to the effects of a Swan trial.

I clear my throat. "Use my blood."

A swan trial is sealed with a sacrifice. The blood used will determine the potency of the spell, and with a little luck, the magic Beth left in me will invalidate the effect of his amulet.

Oz reaches from the interior pocket of his jacket and pulls out an ivory knife. "An immortal's blood would be safest. We don't want to kill the girl." With extreme care, he presses the blade to his wrist. In the disguise of sparring me pain, he's actually protecting his employer.

I ball my fists.

"Use mine," Deveraux announces, stopping Oz short of slashing his arm. Her purple-flecked gaze bores into mine, and she nods ever so slowly. "I'm the host, after all." She marches over to him and holds out her open palm.

The dragon hesitates. "Which one of us will it be, Elsa?" He turns to the Sea Queen who proposed the trial in the first place.

She squints at him. "You are here to protect us and the President. Let Rose make the sacrifice."

Oz gives her a benevolent smile as he passes Deveraux the ivory blade. The professor carves a deep line in her black skin. Blood pours out of the self-inflicted wound, but instead of flowing down to the marble, the stream dances into the air and forms liquid ribbons.

The patrons hold their collective breaths.

"May the lies be exposed. May the liars be tainted," Deveraux says.

"May the lies be exposed. May the liars be tainted," the crowd repeats.

It's the first time in my life that I helped cast a group spell of this magnitude, and the magic takes a life of its own. Power ripples in the air, thick and heavy. The blood swirls above our heads, but I keep an eye on Darkwood. The vampire looks too smug for my taste.

Just as the magic reaches the high of its crescendo, the vampire reaches for his amulet.

The windows of the ballroom explode in a storm of glass. Broken pieces scatter across the glossy marble with a high, tinkering sound. Deveraux cries out in pain and slumps to the ground, her blood raining down on us. Dad dashes over to her.

Lydia runs to the broken windows, her face pale and joyless. "Darkwood turned off the force fields!" she yells loud enough for the entire crowd to freeze in horror.

21

SOMETHING BLUE

Jules

"Rose is injured. I need a healer, quick," Dad commands.

Darkwood raises his hand to Cole. "He blocked the spell."

"*You* blocked the spell. Now turn on the force fields again or everyone here will die!" I cry out. I have this undeniable intuition that if we don't get him now, if we allow him enough time to retreat, we're never going to get another chance.

An ugly pout deforms Darkwood's mouth, and I realize he's counting on it. Whatever happens next, he will pit it on us. Absolute chaos ensues as the guests argue amongst themselves.

Oz's voice booms over the shouts of the crowd. "Get the President and Councilmen out of here! The hollows are coming!"

The magisterium agents clear the crowd to get to their leader, but a solid wall of hollows breaches the confines of the ballroom. They are drawn to magic, and the spell we just cast was of nuclear proportion, which might explain their speedy arrival.

Cole dashes toward Darkwood. "Turn the protective barriers back on, or I'll make sure you die first."

"It's too late now."

Spells zap through the air, and a nasty burn singes my thigh. Darkwood takes this opportunity to act. He moves so quickly, my eyes can't follow, and wraps his arm around my neck.

Magus launch themselves at Cole.

The cold edge of a knife presses on my throat. "Where are the hollows? Tell me."

Most people can't see them, but the white fog slowly divides into individual specters, about ten of them.

"By the windows." A forceful wind blows my hair back as I build an infernal orb in my palm and aim it at his thigh. Deveraux said the amulet protected him from most spells, but I try anyway.

The bastard chuckles. "Now, Miss Winslow. Let's walk together."

The doors at the back of the room slam open as people run for their lives. Screeches blast in the large space, and the distorted sound numbs my ears. Darkwood hauls me closer to the broken windows.

A white eel flies in our direction, unstoppable. Its icy teeth snap at me, and my forehead burns. The creature recoils and whips its tail, apparently stunned for a few seconds.

Holy shit. I'm immune.

Darkwood uses me as a shield as he pushes past the specters. "As soon as you offered up your blood for the ritual, I figured out where my unicorn horn had gone."

I grip his arm and sink my nails inside his skin, but he's as solid as a rock. "Let me go."

The blade at my neck nicks the skin. "Careful now, or we both die."

I will not let Darkwood use me as a piece of armor.

"Let her go." Cole wrestles his way over to us, four Magus unconscious or dead at his feet. His wings are spread on each side of him, and the heavy sting of his powers drums through the air. A flurry of magic-hungry creatures veers toward him.

A black and blue aura shines around him, but no amount of Fae power can save him.

I take a gamble that the hollows are too dumb to sniff out a trap. Instead of an orb, a spike, or any type of weaponized spell, I draw from the very quakes of the earth below my feet and pierce the fabric between worlds.

A burst of heat booms past my cheeks as the fresh underworld tear spreads like wildfire. I just need to put on the biggest show and draw their teeth to us, not Cole. The hollows whip their tails as they approach, jaws clicking in trepidation.

With a loud curse, Darkwood releases me. He jumps over the windowsill and flees into the night, toward the forest.

Cole dashes closer, oblivious to the hollows' presence.

"Don't!"

He frowns but holds himself back in time. The creatures bounce off me one by one, stunned by their unfruitful attack. Lydia advances toward us, her palms wide in front of her, her lips moving quickly. A small barrier stretches in front of her, and she uses it to corral the hollows closer to the tear I built, until the monsters cross to the Underworld.

I hurriedly close the portal, sealing them away. "Let's get the others."

Oz flanks Lydia, searching the room. "Where's Darkwood?" he asks, his face pale, a trail of blood running down his temple.

"Where do you think? The bastard fled," I say.

My dad watches over Deveraux, apparently unharmed.

Allie rises to her feet. "Three or four hollows already buried inside people, so there must be a couple of them left."

Oz nods to confirm her hypothesis.

The ballroom is peppered with bodies, but from afar, it's impossible to distinguish those that were hit by a spell from the unlucky ones who were bitten by a hollow. Brie, Flynn, and Trent are nowhere to be found.

My chest cramps. I don't want to work with the devil, but what else can we do? "Let's take care of the wounded first. We can fight between ourselves afterwards."

Oz chuckles under his breath. "Fine by me."

"Wait! There!" Lydia points to the eastern corner of the ballroom.

We spin around to face the two hollows swimming up to our rear, but Allie, Oz, and Cole blink, unable to see them.

A third hollow gleams under the warm glow of the candelabras. The incorporeal beast is already at top speed, heading straight for Cole's back.

"Cole! Behind you!" I scream in warning, but it's too late.

Lydia desperately tries to push her forcefield forward to stop the beast, but she's too far away.

The creature opens its mouth wide, ready to bite its way inside my husband's body and steal his soul. A dimensional ring stretches behind Cole, and, in a whirl of movement, the specter sinks into Flynn instead.

The forceful blow sends both Fae flying to the ground.

Cole pirouettes to his feet and crouches into a fighting stance while Flynn bites the dust, his body limp on the marble.

Cole's face melts as the weight of what just happened hits him. My heart throbs, my mouth opened in horror. Tears sting my cheeks as I close my eyes, shaking with adrenaline.

"Jules, are you still with me?" Lydia cries out, her gaze still fixed on the two hollows we haven't dealt with yet.

With a nod, I force my attention back to the disgusting monsters and open an underworld tear behind them. Lydia expands her portable force field and advances slowly, until the eels retreat inside the portal.

When I'm sure they're sealed away for good, I run toward Flynn and Cole.

Cole crouches over the blond Fae, in the process of tearing off his red blazer and undershirt.

Strong tremors rock Flynn, and flakes of ice pepper his golden skin. The hollow left a dark line in his stomach where it entered. Cole curls a fist over his friend's torso and punches the ground next to him.

I kneel and grip Flynn's arm.

Cole smoothes his blond locks away from his face. "What were you thinking?" Power ripples off of him in rich, drugging waves.

Flynn smiles and grimaces at the same time. "I missed you, too."

"You should hate me," Cole growls.

"I do hate you. But I love you more."

Sobs quake my chest as I curl my hand over the entry wound.

"Hey, Jules." A painful smile glazes Flynn's blue lips, and sweat gathers on his forehead.

"Hey." I bend over him, and rest my forehead on his.

Cole stands up, his expression unreadable, his fists balled at his sides.

Flynn grazes my cheek. "Don't let him finish me off himself. It'll weigh on his conscience. Get the scary dude—or your Dad."

"What the fuck are you saying?" Cole barks.

With a wince, Flynn tries and fails to sit up. "We both know what needs to happen."

I shake my head. "No."

Oz inches closer. "Darkwood neutralized all the force fields, including the dome that kept the forty-something hollows in the crater from escaping. He wants whatever's inside. We're not safe."

For a moment, I think Cole will actually kill him for saying *we*.

Lydia shakes. "No one should use magic. We can't afford to draw them to us. We need time to rebuild the perimeter."

Forty hollows...

"Stay here and help the others build a new forcefield. I'll catch Darkwood," I say, my heart and hands numb.

Cole grips my lower arm. "I won't let you go alone."

"Stay with him. I'm immune. You're not."

"I don't care. I'm coming with you."

He won't let me go alone. I can see it in his eyes.

Flynn waves us off. "Go. Save the others. I'm past help anyway."

Lydia kneels on the other side of Flynn and cushions his head with her jacket. "I'll stay with him until you return. The hollow won't kill him right away, so there's no need to rush this. We have time—" She buries her face in her palm.

She meant to say that we have time to say goodbye...*before we have to kill him.*

Sharp pain cramps my ribs. "There must be something we can do."

"There isn't. We've tried, but once it's buried inside a host, there's absolutely nothing we can do," Lydia squeaks.

Cole holds up a finger in her direction as though he's about to curse her to hell, but finally nods.

I brush Flynn's hair away from his face and peck his mouth. "We'll be back." I catch a sob from tearing through my lips. "We'll be back and find a way to pull that wretched thing out of your chest, or so help me gods—"

Flynn captures my hand in his and kisses my knuckles. "It's alright, witch. I always knew I'd die for my King."

22

HOLLOWED-OUT

Jules

*A*drenaline prevents me from collapsing as I run to the crater. A gaping hole stands where the thick geodesic dome used to be. The earthquakes remodeled the narrow entrance to the cave, and the winding path I once visited with Beth now slopes down inside the crust of the earth. Cracks and plateaus slowly descend into the depths of Dark Falls, and I send a fire orb forward to see better.

Cole flies over the chasm. "It's too deep for me to see the bottom." He lands next to me along the rim of the hole, and his wings flicker out of view.

I peer over the ledge. "We have to stop Darkwood."

Cole points to a narrow path along the rocks. "There."

A few rocks trickle down the crater under his weight.

"Careful," I say.

"Better me than you. If the ground gives, I can fly."

"Don't use magic," I remind him.

He nods.

I still wish he'd agreed to stay behind. "What if forty hollows are waiting for us at the bottom? Promise me you won't do anything rash."

He threads the path methodically without looking back. "I'm not leaving you here alone."

The earth quakes rapidly under our feet. Shadows and a cloud of smoke obscure the view of the bottom, the crater becoming narrower and narrower as we descend. My heart pounds in my chest, and I flatten my body to the rock wall. Technically, I could survive the fall even if I broke my neck, but I'd be...wrecked.

After a few minutes, the pathway becomes encumbered with rocks. A tunnel forms between the boulders, and I send a second fire orb forward to light our path.

Smoke dries up my throat, and I cough.

Cole maneuvers himself in the tight passage. "It's only a few feet down." He jumps in feet first.

I bend down and glide along the oblique trench. Cole softens my fall, catching me in his arms at the bottom. Roots and dust form a thick carpet at our feet.

"You should let me go first." I dash in front of him.

He clicks his tongue but trails a few steps behind me.

The cave widens in width and height. An archway looms over the now flat path, and ancient alphabet runs along its grooves. Darkwood is immobilized in front of the inscriptions, oblivious to our arrival.

We crouch and slow down the pace.

"Enter here whom has the blood of the phoenix," Cole translates, his chin angled to the inscription. "This is the entrance to Earth's main channel, the one that was destroyed."

"All the more reason to kill Darkwood before he reaches the center."

"But what's 'blood of the phoenix'? Is it just a blanket statement for magic users on Earth? According to the poem in Lydia's book, the phoenix created all supernaturals, including vampires."

"Beats me." I dig my heels in the dirt. "Darkwood is immune to magic. We have to physically stop him."

The vampire's voice echoes ominously in the cave. "Come closer, little witch, and tell me what you see." He points to the space right in front of him.

The space under the archway shimmers with white hues, and I gawk as I realize the strange glimmer is in fact a solid veil of hollows. The incorporeal creatures slither in and out of view, but they don't attack Darkwood. In fact, they remain underneath the arch, guarding the entrance to whatever lays on the other side of the carved inscription.

The hollows hiss as Darkwood stalks closer, and I launch an infernal orb at the rocks above his head, hoping to slow him down. A boulder detaches from the ceiling and forces him to take several steps backwards.

Cole and I rush through the last few feet separating us from him, and my husband pries an obscurion blade from his interior pocket. He runs up to the vampire and aims directly for his heart.

The blow hits, but Darkwood's arrogant smile widens, a yellow-tinged glow emanating from his chest. He grabs the hilt of the blade and wrenches it out of his flesh in a blur.

Cole gapes, taken by surprise, but manages to dash out of the way of the incoming blade, staggering backwards.

Magic and weapons won't harm him...

The vampire raises his eight-point star amulet to Cole. Roots and vines spring out of the earth and weave together to trap him. Cole and I try to blast them away, our red and black magic orbs disintegrating the smaller branches and chopping the thick vines, but fresh ones sprout out of the rocks almost as fast as we can cut them down. A nasty bloom curls around my wrist, and I slice it off with a burst of infernal magic.

The legion of vines wrap themselves around Cole, immobilizing him completely in a chokehold, his head soon the only part of his body visible.

"Stop!"

Darkwood rolls his sleeves up his bony arms. "Now, if you want your beau to survive, you will do as I say. This amulet does a lot, but it doesn't repel hollows. I need your blood to cross this archway Miss Winslow, and only once I'm safe on the other side will I free your precious Fae King."

The high-pitched whines coming from the wall of hollows curdles my blood. The creatures are...suspended in stasis, but their claws and teeth click at my approach.

My heart booms in my chest. "I don't believe you."

"You probably shouldn't." He flashes me his canines.

Cole fights for air in the plant's deadly embrace.

Without thinking, I run full-throttle toward Darkwood, hold my hands and arms straight in front of me, and push him square in the chest. The vampire is strong, but he doesn't weigh a ton, so my momentum is enough to propel us backward.

Darkwood cries out in surprise as I catapult us directly into the wall of hollows. He stabs my neck during the fall, but he can't stop gravity, and we both crash to the ground on the other side of the veil. A deep, frozen sting bites the skin of my arms.

Nails sink deep in my left arm, cutting the flesh, but Darkwood's roar morphs into a painful holler.

Eyes open wide, I watch as one of the incorporeal eel slithers inside the crooked President's heart, and his body hits the dust with a loud *thud*.

I wrench his amulet past his head, and the vines that were choking Cole wither and disintegrate in a *poof* of dust. My husband holds his arms wide on each side of him, catching his breath.

"You okay?" I check on my own injury, but it already started to heal.

Magic sparks off Cole in flares as he nods.

I check on Darkwood again, making sure he's incapacitated, but the hollow wasted no time and already knocked him unconscious.

"Can you haul him back to my side? I'll finish him off myself," Cole croaks. The edges of his body are blurry on the other side of the archway.

"Don't. This is the best case scenario. Darkwood dies without us being officially involved. Let his people finish the job."

I grip the vampire's jacket at the shoulders and slowly drag him back toward Cole. Power thickens and expands my pores. I screw my lids shut and push through the incorporeal creatures. The hollows gnaw and snap at me, but quickly flee with a frustrated hiss. The sting of their cold, desperate hunger frosts my skin, but they begrudgingly slither out of the way, their disappointment palpable. My forehead burns, my skin itchy as hell, the sting a thousand times more pronounced than it was before.

Cole remains at a safe distance from the deadly creatures.

Once I'm safely back on the other side, he uncurls his fists. "Should we take him back with us, then?"

"Let me just check something."

"Wait—" Just as Cole is about to grab my arm, I leap forward and barrel past the veil again.

Beyond it, a solid door carves a passage into the rocks, its surface freckled with rust.

I levitate a fire orb closer to the rusted door. A bronze, dusty insignia decorates its panels, and I walk closer to it. Using my sleeve, I wipe down the insignia to reveal a phoenix. The majestic bird roars with its wings spread on each side.

I turn to Cole. "Allie said Darkwood thought the hollows were protecting a powerful relic. What if whatever lies ahead could cure Flynn and the others? Lydia said I was supposed to get to the source of Dark Falls' power."

Cole paces the antechamber. "It's too dangerous, Jules."

"I need to see what's inside."

"Jules!" He leaps closer to the hollows. Too close. "I'm going to jump."

"You can't."

He raises a brow. "Try me."

"I love you, but I need to do this last part alone. You need to trust me."

"I won't let you run off to your death again." Cole says, one fist knotted in his jet black curls.

"I love you," I repeat, my heart torn in two.

"Damn it, Jules." Vicious tremors rock me from head to toe as he slams his fists to the rock wall behind him, the pulse of his power palpable.

"Wait for me here, it'll only take a minute."

Blood pounds in my ears as I turn on my heels and slip past the rusted door. If someone can follow me inside Dark Falls' hell without any concern for his safety, it's Cole.

I need to hurry.

23

FATES

Jules

The fresh, dry scent of overturned earth tickles my nose. On the other side of the door, a natural cave spreads out in concentric circles. The architecture is a faithful replica of the Fae chapel beneath the Hawthorn, but instead of a black obsidian stone, the centerpiece of the cavern is the six-foot-tall statue of a king.

A crown of bones sits atop his head, his back hunched and his arms spread to the sky, as though he's holding the weight of the entire world on his shoulders.

The statue emits only a faint light, and I build a fire orb to see better. A series of round pedestals spread around the brittle king in a spiral, and a tall, broken mirror stands right behind him. Shattered glass reflects the eerie white light that fills the cave.

A silhouette slowly detaches from a shimmer in the wall, and my heart skips a beat. A long white braid curls over the woman's slender shoulder, her delicate nose and patient expression achingly familiar.

Her appearance is similar to that of Cole's father, the Fae King. He too was there in essence, but not in flesh, and possessed the same ethereal-ness.

"Beth?" I croak.

The woman presses her lips together and shakes her head.

I wipe a tear away with the back of my hand.

"I'm Amalthea, but it warms my heart to meet you, Julia Winslow. Beth lives in you."

The shock subsides. Beth's doppelgänger draws closer, and I notice her silhouette is slightly translucent, and the skirt of her Victorian dress doesn't disturb the dust at our feet.

"You're not actually here, are you?" I ask.

"No, but I felt your arrival."

The layout of the room is similar to where Cole and I got married, and I clutch my necklace. "This place...it's a hall of mirrors. Like the one in Faerie."

"This realm's Hawthorn was destroyed by the Fae King a long, long time ago. To get revenge for burning our most sacred tree and weakening our magic, the Earthly King—" Amalthea raises her hand to the statue—"created and unleashed incorporeal creatures upon his enemy."

"He *made* the hollows?" I stare down the statue again, wondering how one man could be powerful enough to craft a plague—an entire species of monsters—that survived him.

"Yes. He fashioned the very first hollow and sent it after the Fae King, a power-seeking missile of sorts, meant to destroy the most powerful being in Faerie. But after the king died, it mutated into a plague of its own. The creature replicated, each devoured soul fragmenting into two more. We didn't understand what was happening until it was too late."

She walks to the broken mirror. "Earth's main channel had to be sealed off to keep the hollows from annihilating all the magic left in our world. The Earthly King, Ezekiel, hunted them one by one, trying to fix his mistake. After a while, he got so weak that he could no longer destroy them. Instead, he dragged them back here and suspended them in stasis. Unicorns are naturally immune to hollows, so we helped. The last thing he did was to entomb himself with them, hoping to find a way to destroy them for good, but alas, he never completed the task."

She jerks a glance back to the rusted door, and her bottom lip trembles. "The seal held for a millennium. After the Dryad war, the power buried beneath the mountain became coveted. We told them not to dig, that the ghosts buried beneath the earth should be left to rest, but people flock to power, no matter the consequences. They built a school here so that the three realms could share its magic equally, but Malifar, the Underworld King, attacked."

"Beth said many unicorns died protecting Dark Falls..." I say.

"Yes, their deaths fractured the seal, and a few hollows escaped. When your government realized the creatures couldn't be killed, merely contained, they used the underworld portal to send them to Malifar, hoping it would destabilize his reign. All but a few Underworld portals were sealed off after that, leaving the demons to deal with a plague of apocalyptic proportions."

I just used that strategy myself, but I know the Underworld is already swarming with hollows. To think, they just sent them to wreak havoc on demons...

"They just let the hollows kill everyone?"

"Yes."

"The hollows had to be hunted and controlled, but the unicorns were overruled, so we left. Elisheba stayed, hell-bent on guarding these sacred grounds. Somehow, her murder weakened what was left of the seal, and when you took her horn to Faerie—the last remnant of her presence here—it shattered." With a wistful smile, Amalthea shakes her head. "We tried to warn your government, but our speeches sounded like doomsday prophecies to your leaders."

"I don't care about politics. I want to save my friends. There must be a way to destroy the hollows for good. If they were created by a spell, they can be unmade."

"If you're looking for a cure...you're looking at it." She raises her delicate hand to the statue. Light and power ripple through the air as she nears the dusty, understated crown that falls directly over the dead king's brow. "The Aegis...a crown sewn from the bones of the last phoenix, the creature that created all magic-users in this realm."

Sweat sticks to my neck. "I thought the Aegis was a legend."

The proverbial Holy Grail. An object yielding absolute power...

"Legends live and breathe before they become whispers. I'm living proof of that. Are you familiar with the mythos of the phoenix?"

The remnants of the dead king beckon, and I observe the brittle lines in the stone. "Beth wrote about it...Before death, the phoenix sang. Mortals flocked to him, and to thank them, he parted with pieces of himself. It's a beautiful story, a fairytale of sorts."

Amalthea clears her throat. "Before my mother died, she told me a story, too. She said that greed would draw all sorts of creatures to our ancestral lands. She predicted that we would have to abandon them, that monsters would threaten the very fabric of magic in the universe. She was right about it all."

Tingles run up my spine.

Her luminous gaze collides with mine. "She also promised me that, one day, a new phoenix would rise from the ashes of the last. It would come in the shape of a mortal that could cheat death. Magic from the three realms would live inside her, her destiny forged in choices, not just in blood."

"Err—" My heart flutters.

"I didn't think I would live long enough to see it, until Rose and Robert told me about you. A half-demon mortal that was made immortal by Elisheba's gifts. A witch married to a Fae prince..."

"You're saying I'm the linchpin of some prophecy? A...phoenix?"

"You made it here unarmed. You were protected from the hollows by Elisheba's magic and blood from the three realms flows in your veins."

"That doesn't mean—"

"The hollows depend on the Earthly king's magic. To destroy them, one must destroy the Aegis."

My heart beats in my throat. "If I destroy it, will my friends be cured?"

She nods, and my knees buckle. It's too good to be true.

"Why didn't the Earthly king get rid of them? If it was so easy, why didn't he do that instead of herding them here?" I ask.

"Because it will also destroy all earthly magic. Ezekiel couldn't bring himself to do it."

All magic...

"I destroy the Aegis..."

"All the phoenix's magic will drain from the world, yes. Vampires, mermaids, and shifters will become mortal. Witches will no longer command the elements."

I sink my nails inside my palms. "And Fae?"

"Will be left untouched, for their magic has different roots. Your infernal magic, and ours, will also remain."

Still...the thought of going home to a magic-less realm, and being the one to make that humongous choice for all these people...

I want to save Flynn, but at what cost?

Amalthea leans closer. "There is another option. You could also... claim the Aegis and wear the crown. Become the Earthly King."

"You mean queen."

"The word *King* has much more to do with the mystique of magic than gender. You're married to the Seelie King, are you not? But you can't access the well of ancient power that inhabits him. Only he has melded with the Hawthorn, not you. This is similar. Being King is genderless."

I inch forward to touch the crown of bones, my hand trembling.

"If you claim the Aegis, you will be able to touch the hollows. You're young and strong, so you might be able to catch and destroy them all if you made it your life work."

Flakes of dust and ash crumble to the floor as I rub down the legendary crown. The vibrations in the rock still, as though the earth is actually holding its breath. "If I wear this, will I be able to save my friend?"

"I do not know for sure, but I do know that once you wear that crown, you won't be able to change your mind. Once it melds with you, the only way to remove it from your head will be death."

"No pressure, right?" I chuckle darkly. Resentment builds in my belly, a boulder pressing on my diaphragm. "Why didn't you claim the Aegis or destroy it a long time ago?"

"I'm a unicorn. We are gatekeepers, not warriors—and certainly not kings."

A strangled sob bubbles up my windpipe. "I don't want that burden, either."

"You are the phoenix. That can't be helped. You were the one meant to find this crown."

The thin circlet of bones is heavy in my grip, and I screw my lids shut.

To kill or not to kill the magic...

To access a level of power similar to that of the Fae King but condemn myself to a life-long monster hunt, or go for the quicker, straightforward option, and make a choice most people will forever hate me for.

In front of the shattered mirror, I lower the crown over my head, and the brittle bones sink into my skull like wolf's teeth. Static electricity spikes in my hair, and flames engulf me until I'm a living flame.

I was never the one to take the easy way out, and I never lacked ambition. For better or worse, I am King.

24

RISEN

Jules

When I return to consciousness, I pat my head in search of the crown but find only a tangle of red-orange curls. Running my fingers through them, I feel an almost imperceptible circular ridge in my skull.

What the fuck? Did the bones of the phoenix actually meld with mine?

No wonder Amalthea said the crown couldn't be removed without killing me first.

The unicorn is gone, along with the statue of the Earthly King. I stagger to my feet and hurry out the rusted door, praying to all the gods that this won't be another cruel time-jump.

To my extreme relief, Cole is right outside waiting for me.

He paces up and down the space immediately in front of the veil of hollows, seething. "You shouldn't have gone in there without—"

The Fae King squints as I meet his gaze, and my lips curl up in a snarl. Liquid fire covers my palms, the instinct to strike him down imperious. I breathe through the urge to fight my husband to the death, the power inside me crying out for revenge.

"Jules?" he asks, breathless.

"I just need a minute—" My arms shake.

The magic I absorbed clouds my brain, bits and pieces of memory stuck inside of it. I draw in a deep breath and push past the veil of hollows to the other side. They don't sting as they did earlier, but their cold embrace feels emptier still.

A life's work, Amalthea called it…well, if I can kill hollows now, I know which one I want to destroy first.

Cole grazes my hair. "What did you do?"

The bright shade packs a bit of a punch, and I bite my bottom lip. "I…powered up."

He sniffs the air. "The new magic inside you…my gut says not to trust it."

"Same."

The instinct to flee as he sinks his fingers into my hair almost floors me. My chest heaves, and goosebumps freckle my neck. Hatred bubbles up from the Earthly King's memories, but the ache is quickly snuffed out by my love for the Fae King in front of me.

I reach for a kiss, but Cole grabs a fist of my hair and holds me off. "You found the Aegis."

"How do you know?"

"I don't—but the magic in me does. It remembers the Earthly King. It remembers *you*." He licks his lips slowly as though his brain is catching up. "You killed me."

"You burned down my sacred lands."

Cole's lips curl up. "I guess I did." He brushes my hair away from my face and claims my mouth.

The ambivalent punch of our new, elusive memories fogs my brain, but my body recognizes what it loves, and I kiss him back. The Earthly King might have created the hollows to kill a Fae King, but I'll keep this one safe from their ugly teeth, even if I have to spend the rest of my life hunting them down to protect him.

Before he starts tearing my clothes off, I link our fingers and tug gently on his arm. "Come. Let's get the sucker that's buried into Flynn before it's too late."

Cole grows quiet. "You can save him?"

"Maybe. What should we do about Darkwood?" I point to the vampire. Flynn is my priority, and I don't know if I can save one of the hollows' victims, let alone two.

Cole shrugs. "Let his people deal with him."

We hurry back the way we came.

The lights of the ballroom come into view, and Lydia spots us through the broken windows. "Jules!" She jumps over the ledge, carves a door into the thin new force field they erected in our absence, and pulls me into her arms. "You made the right choice, Jules."

"How—"

She hugs me tighter, her voice too low for anyone else to hear. "I saw it, but I couldn't tell you. You're the phoenix." Tears shine in my best friend's eyes as she grazes my new hair.

"Red suits you." She wipes the corner of her eyes and pulls me back to the ballroom, Cole on our heels.

At the entrance, Oz chats with his subordinates.

A parchment and quill fly mid-air next to him, recording everything he says. "We have seven wounded, two dead, and three hollow casualties, but the President is still missing."

An agent runs into the meeting. "We have secured a passage for the healers, boss."

"Well done. Now, we clean out the debris and record the witnesses' testimonies. The High Council will want a detailed recount of what happened here, and how many hollows are—" Oz's gaze flicks to mine, and silence washes over the scene.

"You found the source," he whispers.

"You better not get in my way."

Oz slides to the side to allow us passage. "I was never in your way, Julia. I only did what my superiors ordered me to do."

"That's how you intend to get out of it, isn't it?"

"What if I told you everything I did...the angel fruit theft, the angel dust, killing Elsbeth and framing a Fae prince for it...was all sanctioned by the Senate?"

"I'd say you're bluffing."

He raises his palms to the sky with a disgustingly meek smile. "Maybe I won't get away scot-free, but hey, you probably won't either. Be careful, Julia. Politicians—crooked or not—aren't fond of flashy, powerful witches who make up their own rules."

I want to punch his smug face.

The quill still wiggles happily against the parchment, recording our conversation.

Cole lowers his voice. "Talking of crooked politicians, Darkwood is at the bottom of the crater. He's got a hollow stuck inside him, so if you want a shot in hell at saving your boss, you should hurry."

Oz's face darkens, but he motions for his agents to follow him.

We walk past him and hurry to the center of the room, where stretchers, healers, and grieving guests have started organizing a space for the wounded.

Cole leans closer. "He's right, you know. The Council will not look kindly upon your new powers. A mythical crown combined with a Fae husband...it'll make them nervous."

"Let's worry about that later. It's not like I want to overthrow the government."

"So today was a one-time thing then?" he says with a wink.

Touché...

Lydia guides us to the back of the room where Flynn lies unconscious on a stretcher. "The healers have already assessed him. There's nothing they can do."

Tears mist my vision as I kneel next to him.

"He passed out a few minutes after you left."

The creature is curled around the major blood vessels in his chest like a cancer, a rot slowly spreading from his heart to his brain. I see it plainly, and I realize... it sees me, too.

Hollows aren't exactly rocket scientists, but it senses my arrival.

I press my lips together and square my shoulders to summon the courage to act.

As soon as I reach for the hollow buried in Flynn's chest, he arches his back with a scream. Pain deforms his features and rattles me to my core, but the damned thing holds on, small wisps of its tail planted in the veins and arteries.

I bite back a cringe. "I'm going to need a healer here."

Dr. Chen runs up to us. "Careful, or there won't be anything for me to put back together."

I hiss in pain and continue the delicate task of peeling the hollow out of Flynn without shredding him. Every move coaxes more screams and blood out of him as sweat drips down my back, but I soldier through. My new magic now allows me to *touch* the hollow, slivers of power acting as lassos around its body, allowing me to control its movements. I feel like a kid playing Operation, only hearing the buzzer will kill Flynn.

Once the monster is out in the open, I tighten my fist around its neck, its smokey texture crumbling like sand between my fingers, until there's nothing left.

I feel faint, my mouth dry and bitter.

The healers, Dr. Chen among them, push me aside and tend to what's left of Flynn.

Lydia rests a hand on my shoulder. "There's two more, if you're able."

Despite the power boost of the Aegis, fatigue spreads in my bones. Amalthea wasn't kidding when she said killing hollows required a lot of stamina.

I follow Lydia to the next stretcher where a mortal woman, a witch I've seen a few times on TV, lies on her back.

A second woman cries, hunched over her loved one. "Can you save her?"

I take stock of the woman's condition. Her lips are gray, and the creature wrapped around her heart looks different than the one in Flynn. It's curled up in itself, and a thin membrane covers its skin like a cocoon.

My instincts tell me that, if I try to remove the hollow, the woman will die instantly.

Tears roll down my cheeks. "I'm sorry, it's too late. I can't do anything for her."

Brie grips my wrist, her neon-green hair swirling around her face. "And my mother?"

I follow the mermaid to the Sea Queen, the woman who proposed the Swan trial sitting on a chair.

"You're conscious."

Elsa Demers nods. "Not for long. Brie tells me you might be able to help?"

"The hollow entered through her leg. It doesn't seem to have spread to her chest, yet, though the healers declared her a lost cause," Brie says, her melodic voice brimming with hope.

"Yes, I see it."

The hollow is stuck inside the Sea queen's thigh as though it miscalculated its attack, its white form slowly inching up toward her heart.

I rip it out and kill it. The process takes a few minutes and drains what's left of my energy.

Brie squeezes my hand. "Thank you, Winslow."

I give her a small nod as she kneels at her mother's side.

Cole wraps an arm around my shoulders. "You should take a break. You're white as a sheet."

I rest my head against him for a second. "I'm so tired, I think I could sleep right here."

Dr. Chen hurries to our side. "Flynn is stable now, but unconscious." Her eyes widen at the sight of the cured mermaid.

The entry wound on the Sea Queen's leg has already started to heal.

Dr. Chen licks her lips. "How did you manage to save them?"

"I can touch the hollows."

"What happened to your hair?" Allie's voice resonates behind me.

She stares at me with both hands on her hips, and Dr. Chen slips away to tend to another patient.

Allie squints at Cole and me in turn. "Is it...the *horn* thing?"

Cole pecks my cheek. "I'll make arrangements to have Flynn transferred to the palace. No need to linger on Earth longer than we have to."

I guide my sister to the corner of the ballroom, away from Oz's sneaky quill and the healers' supernatural hearing. "Beth's powers make me impervious to the hollows, so I followed Darkwood to the heart of Dark Falls."

Her mouth opens and closes. "You found the Aegis?" she whispers the last word under her breath.

I check over my shoulder to make sure no one is listening. "Yes."

"Mom told me it was in the cave beneath Dark Falls, but I didn't believe her. Seemed like nothing but a legend."

Legends live and breathe before they become whispers of old...

"Do you hate me?"

"I'm jealous, I won't deny it. But I don't know...it fits you." She motions in the general direction of my head, but I know she's not just talking about the hair.

With a lopsided grin, she points to Mallory and Barron. "They left the library to help with the force fields, the emergency situation taking precedence over Barron's beef with the Magisterium. I should sneak them out of here before the newcomers start asking questions. I'll see you later."

We exchange a quick hug, and I return to Flynn's side, the Fae still unconscious.

A few minutes later, a commotion at the front of the room attracts my attention, and I let go of his hand.

"The President was hit by a hollow," Elsa Demers announces. Her bright-green hair gleams around her face.

I push my way through the crowd of healers and councilmen. The President of the realm lays unconscious on a stretcher in the middle of the huddle.

His demise causes a new wave of panic to wash through the crowd.

Elsa Demers clears her throat. "By Council law, the interim goes to you, Robert. What should we do?"

Piper's high-pitched voice rises in the air. "I must protest. Robert

Winslow is the leader of the opposition. You can't reward his actions here tonight."

"In a state of emergency, if the current elected leader is incapacitated or killed, the highest-ranking Councilman present on the scene takes the reins until a vote can be held," Elsa says.

Piper squeaks. "Again, I must protest—"

"Mom. Stop."

"Allison."

Dr. Chen raises her voice. "Julia Winslow saved Elsa Demers and the Fae. Maybe she can save the President, too."

Dad traces the line of his brow. "Can you help him, Munchkin?"

I hold back a sigh. Am I really going to save Theodore Darkwood from a sure, swift death? The crowd parts for me, and I walk over to the old vampire.

He writhes on the thin stretcher, his white skin almost translucent, his wrinkles deep enough for sweat to gather into the cracks.

"Give her some space," Lydia shouts from the side.

Inspired by her outburst, the four Magisterium agents flanking the President clear out the crowd, allowing me to breathe.

Trent kneels next to his father, and while a certain level of anguish shows on his face, he's not at all the picture of a grief-stricken son.

The brown-haired vampire offers me a sad smile as I join him. "Nice hair."

"Err—Thanks."

We both observe his dying father, and I swallow hard, undecided about what to do.

Trent gives my arm a gentle squeeze. "Maybe it wouldn't be so bad if the hollow had already done too much damage...if we had to put him out of his misery. Maybe it's already much more than he deserves."

The true meaning of his words passes between us.

I bite my lips and take stock of the damage done to Theodore Darkwood, President of the realm, and the devil whose schemes derailed my life.

"It's too late for him," I say loud enough for everyone to hear.

Trent lets out a long—but relieved—breath. "That's what I thought."

25

THE WIZARD

Allie

The chaos of the attack somewhat subsided, but seeing Daniel organize his troops and tend to the wounded like he's fucking Mother Theresa sets me on edge. I thoroughly avoid the corner where Melanie and Trent stand and cross the room to speak with my father.

Before I escort Barron and Mallory outside, I need to make sure of something.

"Hey, are you okay, Peanut?"

"You have to tell Jules about Mallory." I squeeze his lower arm to punctuate my statement, letting him know that I mean it.

Wrinkles appear at the corner of Dad's eyes. "How did you know?"

"I know you."

He scratches his neck, eyes cast down. "I'm not proud of it, but if

I'd tried to do more for Mallory, Jules would have been in grave danger."

"I understand, and she will too. Tell her."

I thought I was like Piper, but I'm actually more like him. Ambitious, but to a point. Willing to sacrifice innocents if needed, but ready to die to protect my family. I just need to not let narcissistic assholes into said family.

"I will. Not here, but as soon as we're alone. I promise."

Revelations about Mallory's true identity should come from him, not me. I can't believe my little sister, the one who would always shriek during horror movies, has claimed the Aegis, the most powerful relic on Earth.

"We need to come up with a plausible lie as to how she managed to cure Elsa Demers and Flynn. No one should know she has the Aegis," I say.

If that new power of hers can be stolen, I'm sure many supernaturals would kill for such a treasure.

Mother lurks closer, her eyes red and her perfect nails in shambles.

"Robert...I think your daughter lied about Theo's chances. I demand a second opinion."

A big frown twists my face. "Mom. Stop."

Is she serious? No one else could provide a *second opinion,* and even if they could, what good would it do?

Dad pinches the bridge of his nose. "Here's what's going to happen, Piper. You and Allie will provide the Magisterium with all the details surrounding Elsbeth Eillis' murder. Tell them Darkwood came up with the plan and enlisted Osbourne to carry out the deed. It'll be easy to prove his part in it, but if we're not careful, Osbourne will weasel his way out of charges because of his subordinate relationship with the ex-President. With your testimony, and Allie's, we can nail him."

Mom grows a shade whiter. "I won't—"

"Without the amulet Darkwood stole to protect you..." Dad trails off softly, almost regretfully. "You must think long and hard about how you want the world—and your only child—to remember you."

"Robert..."

172

"I'm sorry Piper. I truly am. You also have to decide who should be the one to put Darkwood out of his misery." Dad squeezes my hand before walking away.

Tears sting my eyes, but I won't let them fall. Mom is condemned without the amulet, and that part *sucks.*

"We should consult with my lawyer—"

"It's over, Mom."

She convinced me we could conquer the world together, but she sold her soul to Darkwood and mine along with it.

I head over to Barron. The duo helped Lydia build a new perimeter after the initial attack, and Mal is still chatting with the redhead.

The Scot's dimmed his shadowy aura. His hands are tucked deep in his pockets, his shoulders hunched like he wants to downplay his height and avoid attention. If it wasn't for the chaos of the last few hours, I don't think he would have shown his face here.

"You got your revenge, Little Storm," he murmurs.

"Did I?"

He scratches the nape of his neck. "Mal wants to visit Faerie with your sister and her husband. They apparently go way back, even though she was a cat then. I'm going to set sail tomorrow morning and meet up with my twin brother, Lucas. Yer welcomed to join, if ye want."

My throat dries up, the invite a surprising one to say the least. "I'm needed here."

He gives me a sharp nod. "Don't let politics ruin yer life."

"That's all you have to say?"

Doesn't he remember his promise? Is he only attracted to me when I'm boiling with rage?

As if on cue, Daniel taps on my shoulder. His sudden closeness makes my head spin. "I need to speak with you."

Barron's dark aura thickens, but he doesn't move an inch.

Daniel glides his hand down my arm and guides me aside. His sheepish grin turns my stomach.

"Come on now, kitten. I didn't know you were alive. I swear."

"We were both played, then."

"Doesn't it make you squirm? Your sister gets power, recognition, immortality…"

I know what he's doing. He wants to stoke my envy. Maybe he means to shock me to regain my trust…or he just likes to see me suffer.

I meet his gaze head-on. "Better to get nothing than to get screwed." I shiver, because despite my anger and his treachery, a part of me still yearns for his approval, and it disgusts me.

He probably only wants to get back into my good graces because of Dad's new position.

"You never loved me, did you?"

He shakes his head in disbelief. "Don't play the victim, here. You're a clever, ambitious girl. You knew what you were signing up for."

Before I can stop myself, I punch him square in the face. He recoils, holding up his hand to shield his eyes. My silver ring left a dent in his brow.

He licks his lips. "I admit I deserved that. See you later, kitten." He spins on his heels with a wink like this is merely a time-out, and I'm condemned to gravitate his orbit.

Maybe I have it all wrong.

Barron's large frame towers behind me as I watch Daniel leave. "He can't own you, if you don't let him."

"Does vengeance always taste so bitter?" I choke.

"Ye have no idea…" the words are both wistful and dark.

A new ambition rumbles in my belly.

Daniel Osbourne is right about one thing. I'm not a victim, or at least I don't want to stay in that role. If he used me and manipulated me…I won't let it become my pattern.

I can't let Jules play with fire alone. And if my sister has already achieved immortality and a fate that'll put her name on everyone's lips, despite all odds, who says I can't do the same?

"You live for revenge… Teach me." Barron might call himself a druid, but he's a warlock first. There's no reason why he shouldn't be able to teach me his brand of magic. If the spell he used tonight is any indication, the treasures buried below deck must be enough to change the course of history.

He rubs the curve of his jaw. "I thought you weren't into lowly scavengers."

I summon a confidence I don't possess yet and grab a fist of his shirt to pull him down for a very scandalous, very public kiss. "As it turns out...I've got a thing for scoundrels."

26

DARKER DEALS

Jules

Dead pine needles crunch under my bare foot, but the unending forest is quiet. The woods feel different, the mud at the foot of the trees smells different, but I try not to let my senses distract me from my task.

"Are we close?" Cole asks, surveilling the darkness like he expects Darkwood's ghost to attack us.

"We're almost to the center."

Wearing the crown has rewritten parts of my memory, and I recognize every rock slab and every ridge of the mountain.

Cole slips his fingers in mine. "We could have done this another time. You're still figuring out your new powers, and killing hollows took a lot out of you."

"It'll only take a minute." Less than two days have passed since the show-down with Darkwood, but I need to do this *now*. As long as the Underworld tear exists, I won't be able to sleep properly.

I guide Cole through the trees until we reach the epicenter of the earthquake—the origin of the timesink that sucked parts of the academy into another world.

The rapid throbs of the earth under my feet call out to me, and I crouch to touch the ground. I can feel the void below Dark Falls clearer than ever before. The crater bleeds at the edges, the entire fabric of our realm stretched thin.

I close my eyes and let the pain flood through me, feeling every inch of the tear.

Small stones quake near my feet as I draw in a deep, controlled breath and press my palms to the ground. My new powers build in my palms until the void below us, a void that stretches for miles beneath Dark Falls, seals itself back in one breath.

It's frighteningly easy—no harder than twisting a lock with the right key.

The air stills for a moment, and the peace that follows coaxes a sigh of relief out of me.

Here, old friend. You can rest now.

"You did it, Jules. You closed the biggest tear in history."

I press my lips together. "It wasn't as hard as I thought it'd be. I just have the right set of tools, I guess."

A smile warms his handsome face. "Don't sell yourself short. What you just did is extraordinary." He holds his arm out to escort me back to Faerie. "Now, your Kingdom awaits, my queen."

He zaps us to his hall of mirrors, and we hike up to his apartments. His sister Helena planned a big party to celebrate my return, but I'm not in the mood.

I visit Flynn in the convalescence room we organized next to Cole's office.

A team of shamans watches over him day and night, but it's been *days*, and he still hasn't woken up.

"Any change?" I ask the shaman.

The old Fae crushes a few sage leaves with a mortar and pestle as he shakes his head. "He's still unconscious, but every spell tells us he's recuperating. It shouldn't be long now."

I'm terrified that I messed up when I tore the hollow out and that Flynn suffered permanent damage. His rhythmic breaths tickle my ears as I sit on a chair next to him and grip his hand.

Flynn's fingers twitch in mine, and his breathing pattern changes ever so slightly.

My heart stops. I lean forward and check for any sign of consciousness, but he slips back into his earlier state.

Cole wraps his arms around me. "He just needs time to heal."

My superstitious side urges me to remain cautious. "We should wait before having a party."

He places a sweet kiss at the nape of my neck. "Our people need some good news. They want to see their queen, alive and well. This isn't about dancing or having fun, but celebrating your return and cementing our intention to rule together. Flynn will understand, and we can celebrate our victory when he's better."

"Still..." I stand up and face him.

He cups the side of my face. "It's only a party, and I'll be standing by your side the whole time."

I hug him close, his heat melting my fears. "Alright."

"Am I invited to this party?" Flynn croaks behind me.

A hiccup shakes my throat. "You're awake." I scurry to his side and squeeze his hand.

He blinks, his lids heavy. "Hey, witch."

A breath of relief rumbles through my entire body as I brush a blond lock away from his baby-blue eyes. Cole inches closer, his arms crossed.

"Welcome back," he grunts under his breath like the words are costing him dearly.

Flynn shuffles in his bed, propping his head up with a pillow. "Still grumpy, I see."

A dark chuckle grates through Cole's throat. "Don't sacrifice yourself for me again, and I won't have to be so grumpy."

Flynn tilts his chin up from his hospital bed, his gaze lethal. "I will sacrifice myself for you *as many times as it takes*."

I'd laugh if it wasn't for the charged energy in the air. When Flynn gets out of bed, I'm not sure if my men are going to fight or fuck, but I know it'll be violent either way.

"You two are just going to have to make nice," I say.

"Yeah—"

"Well—"

"—don't count on it," they add in unison.

I grin at the synchronized response. "Why did you guys fall out? Neither of you really explained what happened. Not in a way that would explain your behavior, anyway."

They both retreat deeper into themselves, and I roll my eyes at their stubbornness.

"Fine. I'll share my theory first. I think both of you reacted to your grief differently, and instead of growing closer, you took out your emotions on each other until you couldn't stand to be in the same room together." I take a dramatic pause, watching their reaction. "How am I doing so far?"

"He called me a worthless drunk," Flynn says.

Cole turns his back to the bed, running a hand through his curls. "You showed up wasted to an operation and almost got everyone there killed—including you. If that wasn't the most moronic—"

"Nothing mattered to you anymore besides that damn war...not even me. You posted me as far away from you as you possibly could."

Cole snickers, the sound dry and unkind. "I didn't want you to get beheaded between two bottles of gin."

Flynn props himself up on the bed, holding his weight with his hands. "Ohhh, you did me a favor, did you?"

"Absolutely."

... At least they're talking?

"That's bullsh—" Flynn moves to stand up, but his face pales to a sickly, paper white shade.

"You should rest." I motion for Cole to leave and help Flynn settle back into the bed.

With a big wince, he curls his fists over the edges of his mattress. "Fuck. That thing really ripped me to shreds."

The shaman bows quietly as he approaches his patient, his brows pulled together in one thick line. "He needs more sleep, and quiet, or the pain will return. Let me get you a sedative."

"Just rest for now. I'll be back soon."

Flynn motions loosely to my head. "Are we going to talk about your hair?"

"I change color all the time," I say with a quick, humorous shrug.

A light chuckle warms his face. "True enough."

"I was afraid you'd never wake up."

"I'm here, witch."

We exchange a quick kiss, and I leave my patient to the shaman's expertise.

When I return to the bedroom, Cole has already started to change into the clothes Helena prepared for us. After taking a quick shower, I join him by the bed. A thundercloud still drapes his features in shadows, his mouth curled down.

"Are you okay?" I ask.

"You have no idea how stupid he acted while you were gone," he says, adjusting his tie.

I discard my towel and slip the black dress over my head. "It's Flynn. I think I have *some* idea."

Sequins weigh down the skirt of the dress, but the shiny embellishments grow sparse around the waist and only pepper the button-down neckline.

A sigh blows through my husband's mouth, his gaze fixed on the corner of the room. "It's like he was trying to kill himself by accident —and everyone around him."

I walk over to him and stroke his shoulder over his black button-down shirt, the edges of his scars visible over the turned-down collar. "It's okay to be upset. Give it time."

Cole pries a big jewelry box from his closet, clears his throat and angles it toward me.

I bite my bottom lip. "What is it?"

He smiles mysteriously as I open the box. Copper, silver, and gold threads, arranged to resemble roots, form an elegant, absolutely beautiful crown set with rows and rows of precious stones.

My breath hitches. "Cole, it's…"

"Yours." He helps me put it on right, over my wild, colorful curls.

I stand on the tip of my toes to kiss him. "Thank you. It's perfect."

A discrete tear shines in his eyes, and his gaze darts to the ground for a split second. "I never thought I'd feel like this again…"

"Like what?"

"Happy."

I link our fingers. Shadows caress the foliage of the Hawthorn, moonlight bathing the interior courtyard as well as the king's bed. Our gazes lock, the burning sensation in my chest growing into a dizzying pressure.

"You came back and took it all in strides, and even though I have been here, been King, for a decade, my entire world suddenly feels… completely different."

Eyes closed, I press my forehead to his. "I feel that way, too."

Cole crushes me to the window with a searing kiss. "A part of me still wants to kill you, you know? Just letting you this close to the Hawthorn…" his hands shake on my hips.

"I know. I kinda want to burn it," I say, half-teasing, half-not.

He wraps a soft hand around my throat and kisses my neck. "Don't joke about that."

"The distrust between the Kings is ancient history. The magic will just have to get on board with its new reality."

We make out until we're both out of breath. I'm back to kissing my nemesis, but I remember this feeling all too well when it comes to Cole, and I don't hate the familiar thrill in my bones.

He grips my ass and presses me hard against his erection, ready to make me his again. "I wasn't kidding when I said I wasn't the same as before." He holds both arms above my head, and the metallic foliage above the windows suddenly snake along the glass to snatch my wrists.

His amber eyes pulse in the night. "I'm darker."

"I want it darker."

Cole slides his hands down my bound arms to the buttons at the front of my dress, working it open. "I'm going to make you beg for forgiveness, Earthly King."

"I'd never beg a Fae King," I answer in jest.

"Is that a challenge?" He pulls his shirt over his head, and the shape of his bare shoulders sends a hot flash of desire through me.

"Do we have time?" I bite my bottom lip, calculating what leeway we have before Helena wants us both dead.

"It's our party. We can be fashionably late."

My gaze dips to his abs and the v-shaped groove of his adonis belt. "I'll make you a deal."

"A deal? Are you sure?" He glides his hands to the back of my thighs and pulls the skirt of my dress above my hip.

"We're going to hunt down the hollows *and* the Unseelie—starting with the one that hurt you. *Together.*"

He boosts me up, allowing me to wrap my legs around him. The tip of his nose glides along the slope of my neck as he works open his belt. "Alright."

The soft *swish* of fabric echoes deep in my belly.

"Yeah?"

He squeezes the nape of my neck. "By the Dark Gods, I swear it."

He plants a long, sensual kiss on my lips as he enters me. Every slow thrust flattens my back to the cold glass, my core dripping with fire, and I know immortality will not be long enough to quench my thirst for him.

27

QUEEN

Jules

*A*fter our unplanned tryst, we smooth down our hair and clothes and descend the stairs to join our guests in the ballroom. Music seeps through a large crowd, the atmosphere allowing for conversations and cocktails more than dancing. The checkered floor gleams under the light of large, tiki torches.

"Every Fae Lord and Lady is in attendance," Cole whispers in my ear.

I watch the crowd for a familiar face but there are simply too many Fae courtiers. "Aren't some of them conspiring against you?"

His lips quirk. "A few, but that will change tonight if I can help it. I made a point to ask my mother to behave, so she shouldn't give us any grief."

Celeste Draco. Ugh. The ex-headmistress already tried to have me killed and expelled, so I'd rather not have to exchange pleasantries with her tonight.

Helena opens her arms in greeting. "Welcome to your back-from-the-dead party." A purple satin dress hugs her voluptuous curves, and a long, flashy shawl is wrapped around her elbows. A big, mischievous grin twists her face as she pecks us both on the cheek. "Do you like it?"

The flippant and macabre theme showcases shades of black, green, and purple. A multitude of caskets hang from the ceiling, as though we are actually buried underground.

A waiter dressed in an over-the-top zombie costume hands me a champagne flute, and I try not to gawk as I pick it up.

Cole clicks his tongue. "I asked you to keep it simple."

"When have I ever planned something *simple*? I figured we should embrace the creepiness of the situation. Don't worry, I have planned the boring and cliché royal wave from the balcony and asked the guests to show up in their best styles. This isn't some cheap, zombie party. It's a voodoo *fête*." She raises her arms to the sky, and a throng of red, gold, and purple feathers trickle down from the ceiling.

"It's memorable, that's for sure," I grumble, taking a sip of champagne.

"You see? She likes it."

Cole shakes his head, eyes shining with humor. "That's not what she said."

Helena sticks her tongue out. "Gratitude is a virtue, little brother. Now, come and chat with my friends."

Lydia wades her way through the crowd, Trent and Mallory a few steps behind her.

I wave for Cole to follow his sister. "Go. I'll join you in a minute."

I hug my best friend, breathing a little easier now that she's here. "Thank you for coming."

"I figured you might need some back-up."

Mallory gives me a small wave, her long brown curls braided over her slender shoulder. "Hey, Jules."

She's got the most peculiar expression on her face, like she's... excited to see me.

"Hey, Mal. I'm glad you decided to stay. You, me, and Cole can have a chat later about how to involve you in our plans."

She nods. The demon wants to help us navigate the Underworld, and now that she's no longer cursed, she probably hopes to find her people again, though we haven't had the time to get into the details.

"My queen." Trent bows with a goofy smile on his face. He's ditched the Fae soldier uniform in favor of a jacket and tie.

I slap his arm playfully. "Stop it."

The vampire skims Lydia's waist. "I'm going to get a drink. Do you girls want something?"

We all shake our heads, and I give my best friend a knowing glance.

Blood pools on her cheeks. "Don't start. We're just friends."

"Mm-Mm." I wiggle my brows, barely holding a chuckle in, and Lydia elbows my side. I force myself to sober up. "Have you guys... talked?" I motion between my two friends, remembering the time Onyx almost ripped Lydia to shreds.

"You mean, did I forgive her for being cursed into an evil cat form as a child and almost scaring me to death? Well, I could hardly hold that against her, could I?"

We all share a laugh, and things almost feel...normal again.

"What's going to happen to Dark Falls now that the tear is closed?" I ask.

Lydia's green eyes shine with hope. "Deveraux accepted the Council's offer to become headmistress. Trent and I will help her whip the school into shape. The next batch of students won't benefit from some mysterious power underground, but they'll have good teachers —and a better chance at survival."

"That's good."

"What about you? Are you really going to hunt down *all* the hollows left?"

I gulp down what's left of my drink and discard the empty flute on a nearby table. "Yep. One by one. The Magisterium will corral those that escaped on Earth while we find a way to take down the Unseelie hub in the Underworld."

"And I'll help," Mal adds.

Lydia squeezes my shoulder. "I'll be there, too, whenever you need me."

"Thank you. Both of you." I say, my voice muted by the burst of emotions threatening to floor me. Cole and I found each other again, Flynn is okay, Dark Falls is safe… I can finally, *finally* breathe again.

Mal surveils the crowd. "Allie and Barron will be sorry they missed this."

"Allie's been through a lot. She deserves a bit of time to find herself without her life revolving around me."

The light music dies down, and all heads turn to the entrance. My father is there, and he straightens his jacket at the top of the stairs. To my horror, Oz follows right behind him, along with a second Magisterium agent. Both of them are wearing the traditional black and gold uniform.

Cole joins us almost immediately.

"The nerve! Why would he show his face here?" Lydia says through her teeth, echoing my current sentiment.

I'm simply shaking with rage. "What. the. Fuck."

"Your father ordered him to come. He asked Oz to be responsible for his personal security tonight."

My heart pulses in my throat. "What? Why?"

"It was my idea. Trust me." He guides me forward to greet my father, the current President of the realm. The whispers flurrying through the crowd confirm my hunch that it's in fact a big deal for him to come to such an event, and I might gush about inter-realm cooperation if I wasn't so pissed to see Oz.

The dragon doesn't look half as smug as I expect him to be.

"Welcome to Faerie, President Winslow," Cole says with his most congenial voice.

Dad smiles. "I was pleased to receive your invitation, and I brought the gift you asked for."

Both men shake hands, their smiles a little too wide to feel normal, before Cole's gaze turns downright predatory.

He signals for his guards to step closer. "Daniel Osbourne, you're under arrest."

Oz stiffens and takes a few steps back. "Fuck you, Winslow. I knew you were planning something. I should have never set foot in this wretched realm," the dragon grits though his teeth.

"You made a point to repeat that you couldn't disobey direct presidential orders," Dad says cheekily.

Oz shoves the first guard away but is quickly immobilized by two others. "And what I am being arrested for?"

An unkind grin stretches Cole's lips. "Framing me for murder? Conspiring with my enemies to dethrone me? Take your pick."

"You will have to let me stand trial on Earth. Our laws make sure of it."

"Yes, but you'll have to think long and hard about your sins before that day comes. As I'm sure you're aware, Faerie has prisons where time is...let's say...fucked up."

"I just hope I live long enough to see your kingdom burn, elf," he seethes as the guards take him away.

Lydia shakes her head in disbelief. "Man. Allie would have loved to see that."

Vindication sizzles in my blood, but a muted sense of caution rears its head. "Are you sure arresting Oz won't create some sort of incident?"

"He'll only be gone a few weeks...or at least *for us*, it'll only be a few weeks," Cole says.

My gaze darts from Cole to my father and back again. "I can't believe you two planned this together."

"We figured he still might be acquitted in his trial. We decided he deserved worse."

"Oh, he deserves *the worst*," I say.

Dad nods, and I realize the animosity he felt towards Cole, toward my choice to become his wife, was melted by the years I missed. He looks me up and down with muted reverence, like he can't believe that I'm me. "I'm proud of you, Munchkin. I just returned the amulet to Amalthea, and she told me all about...you know. I think you made the right choice."

My eyes mist, a bonfire of emotions burning in my heart.

"That means a lot. I love you, Dad." I press my lips together, suddenly thinking of Allie and her mother. "But if you gave the amulet back, doesn't it mean that Piper..."

His face grows somber, and he nods slowly, almost regretfully. "Piper has been cheating death for years, and she did so at the expense of other people's lives. She knows what she needs to do, now."

I swallow hard.

Helena walks over to us. "Enough drama, it's time to greet our people."

"You love drama, sis," Cole says.

A pout purses her painted lips. "Not when it's politics."

"Are you ready, Fire Girl?"

I draw in a deep breath. Am I ready to meet his people as their queen? Deafening applause slips through the large double doors leading to the balcony as Helena announces our arrival to the masses. Judging by the sound, thousands of Fae citizens have flocked into the streets of Mellen to catch a glimpse of us.

Cole squeezes my hand. "Don't worry, they're going to love you."

I swallow hard, aware my husband just got to the crux of my anxiety. It's one thing to yield the power of the Earthly King, but it's an entirely different burden to have the eyes of a thousand Faerie citizens fixed on me...to know they are counting on us to stop a war that decimated their families.

"You were meant for this, Jules Winslow." He tugs gently on my arm.

Nerves buzzing in my belly, I pat down my head, making sure my crown is not crooked. "How are you so confident?"

A dimple appears in his cheek. "Because I *see* you."

AN UNDERWORLD MAP is propped over my thighs the next morning as I study the ins and outs of the continent and the probable location of its Hall of Mirrors. Cole's office is a little chilly, and I tighten my jacket around my frame before a soft thud alerts me to Mallory's arrival.

"Jules, are you in there?" the demon asks, peeking through the doorway.

I wave for her to join me. "Yes. Maybe you can help me, I'm trying to pinpoint the location of the Underworld hub. Cole went to the library for the old maps, but this doesn't make sense."

"Actually, I have something to show you." She bites her lip, her voice a little higher than before. "I didn't want to bring it up yesterday because you had so much on your plate, but... Barron gave me something before he left."

I discard the map of the table. "What's up?"

"He kept this below deck all these years...an heirloom I inherited from my mother." She opens the velvet bow, and I hold my breath as an exact copy of my emerald necklace comes into view.

"But it's—" I clutch the pendant hanging between my breasts. "Does this mean we're—"

Tears pool in her brown eyes as she grazes the precious stone. "I think so. I was always meant to find you, Jules. We're *sisters*."

Sisters... my arms shake, but Mallory steadies them and wraps me in her embrace. We hug each other for the longest time, my thoughts too fast for my brain to catch up.

"Do you remember her? Our mother?" I say on a sniffle.

A sob escapes her, her curls grazing my cheek. "Bits and pieces."

We slowly regain the ability to breathe normally. I wipe a tear from the corner of my eye and walk to the desk for a fresh tissue.

"I found it!" Cole dashes back from the library holding a roll of parchment, oblivious to our revelation.

He lays down a new map over the ones already scattered on his desk and draws a circle with his fingers over a crescent-shaped lake. "Here. The books on the Underworld hub mentions a body of water shaped like the smile of the moon. We should start there."

Mal clears her throat and looks over his shoulders. "I agree."

I tap the representation of Dark Falls on the ginormous map, the shock of Mallory's revelation slowly morphing into excitement and joy...*no wonder she was so happy to see me yesterday.* "I still want to test the main channel and make sure it's reliable before we go gallivanting around a hollow-infested continent."

"Hollows don't intimidate me anymore. As long as we don't get separated, they won't be able to hurt us. The Unseelie on the other hand...we'll need an army for them." Cole cracks his knuckles.

"Once we find the hub, we can gather an army. Isn't that your specialty?" I tease.

"Most Fae don't have infernal magic and the power of the phoenix to rely upon."

I wiggle my brows. "Are you bothered by the fact that I'm more powerful than you now?"

The corners of his mouth curl up. "Who says you're more powerful?"

"She is, though," Flynn cracks, joining us through the opposite door. I open my mouth to speak, but he raises his index finger. "Don't start. The shamans gave me a clean bill of health."

He swapped his white Fae shirt for jeans and a black sweater, and he looks damn fine in it, despite the few bruises still visible on his neck. I walk over to him for a quick kiss, relieved to see him standing strong so quickly.

The boys exchange a tensed glance, but neither of them seems inclined to fight...for now.

Flynn spots the maps on the desk and rubs his palms together. "So? What's the plan, here? Who's ass should we kick first?"

I let out a tearful chuckle. "Before we decide *that*, there's something Mal and I need to tell you both."

28

HALO

Cole

The Hawthorn bristles in the dark garden. Its leaves ripple at the strong wind, their oily underside shimmering in the night.

Jules slips out of bed and joins me by the window. "Hey. What's going on?"

Flynn's light breaths echo through the bedroom. Despite our sleeping arrangements, I haven't forgiven him. The bastard sacrificed himself for me, making it harder to hold on to my grudge. Leave it to Flynn Verinos to find new ways to crawl under my skin.

"I'm still angry with him."

"No? Really?" Jules says in jest.

She wraps her arms around my bare midriff and kisses my back, the silk of her nightgown cool on my bare ass.

Greed burns at the back of my throat, and my heart gives a powerful thud. She's mine, and with her, the power of the Earthly King. The thought alone is enough to make me hard again.

I twist in her embrace. The orange tint of her hair has faded in the last few weeks. Purple and black locks balance her new phoenix look.

"Why are you staring at me like that?"

"Shh." I nibble her pulse point, and she simply melts in my arms.

I'm ravenous for her. A decade in withdrawal only solidified my addiction. Her touch, her taste, the breathless moans of pleasure she can't keep to herself...I can't get enough.

The periwinkle nightgown hugs her delicious curves, and I drag it up to her lower back and press my erection to her core.

She shakes her head like I'm being totally unreasonable, but falls to her knees in front of me. Gods.

I wrap her hair in my fist as she strokes me up and down and wraps her beautiful lips around the head of my cock. My hips buck, but I fuck her mouth with long, slow thrusts. Hard nipples show through the silk of her nightgown, and my abs tighten at the sight.

I glance up and meet Flynn's gaze across the room.

He licks his lips and raises a brow. He knows he's not back in my good graces, and while my knee-jerk reaction is to tell him off, I motion for him to approach.

His throat bobs as he shuffles off the bed, his long cock already throbbing in anticipation.

"Strip her," I bark.

Jules sucks me harder, the scent of her arousal so potent that I hiss.

Flynn works the straps of her nightgown down her arms, and her heavy, perfect breasts come into view as the fabric pools at her hips.

I tug on her hair, pulling out of her mouth in the process, and angle her face to Flynn. "I want you to tease him until he begs for mercy."

"And you..." I walk around the lucky bastard and hold his wrists behind his back. "You will not come until I say so."

Tremors run through Flynn, his biceps straining, but he nods.

I can't help it. Angry or not, seeing them together riles me up. It makes me feel both competitive and so fucking horny...especially when they act out my orders, both happy to indulge my hunger for dominance.

She traces the length of him with her tongue before taking him inside her mouth. Our eyes meet, and the love and lust in her heated gaze is almost enough for me to root for this...thing we have going on. Almost.

"Oh—fuck." Flynn struggles against my hold, but I only tighten my grip. His butt clenches against my erection as she takes him right to the edge. "I'm close."

"Not. Yet."

She sneaks a hand between his legs to stroke me, driving me wild.

I release Flynn and pick Jules up off the ground, ready to claim what's mine. "Enough." I kiss the hollow of her neck. "Let him suffer."

"Fuck you, Cole."

A dark grin escapes me at the sincerity of his outburst. "Take care of it yourself, then."

The bed plies under our weight as I climb over Jules and fuck her senseless. Her nails dig into my shoulder blades as I give her what she craves, in the exact way she needs it. Her breaths become shallow and uneven, and her thighs quake on both sides of me. I cup her ass and hold her to me, giving her the pressure she goes mad for, her pussy so tight and slick around my cock that I forget where I am for a moment.

Flynn strokes himself in perfect synch with my thrusts, the pinch of his pace telegraphing how close he is to his climax.

Her wall spasms around me as she cries out in bliss, her back arched against the bed. I run a hand down the length of her body, riding out her orgasm until she blinks and smiles wickedly.

Fuck.

"I want you both to come *on* me." She arches a brow that dares me to deny her.

I pull out of her and wrap a hand around my painfully engorged cock. By the Dark Gods, I'm going to burst.

Jules holds herself up with her elbows and motions to the space between her breasts.

Flynn and I exchange a glance, and a hot line of anger sizzles along

193

my spine, my competitive side unsure if it's a race to the finish line, or a show of stamina. Fuck, I don't think it matters, the skin at the back of my balls tingles with fury.

With a sharp intake of breath, I fulfill my wife's wish, Verinos climbing to her side, both of us now with her on the bed. Our seeds spread and mix over her smooth, tanned skin, and the sight is outrageous enough for me to groan and shove him away.

I crash next to Jules on the bed, pleasure rippling through my body. We all catch our breaths, our chests heaving. Gods. Over the years, I tried to convince myself that I had amplified our mental and physical connection. Many told me I had merely put Jules on a pedestal, and that I was letting nostalgia control my life, but they were wrong.

When I'm with her, I'm...more. More powerful, more patient, more forgiving, more open.

She makes me better and steals my breath at the same time.

I grumble as Jules heads for the bathroom, leaving no neutral ground between Flynn and me, and I spin around to face the other way.

"You've got issues, you know?" he whispers angrily.

I stare dead ahead. "Why are you sleeping in here again?"

"Cut to the chase, *your highness*. Why are you so fucking grumpy? Are you jealous because Jules nursed me back to health? That we had sex? What?"

"No."

"Then what is it? Do you still care for me at all?" his voice breaks at the end.

It awakens all the fucked up guilt I'm carrying.

"I—" I sink my nails in the pillow, holding on for dear life. "I'll always care for you."

"I mean—beyond our history? If not, I should leave."

I spin around and throw a pillow at his face. "You gave your life for me. We both know you had no hope of a cure...How am I supposed to live with that?"

Silence hangs between us for a few, long seconds, and Flynn's gaze softens. He inches closer to me. "You saved me, too. A thousand times over."

"Pfft."

"Mostly from myself, my damn big mouth, the ocean of self-loathing inside my heart..." He moves to touch my hand but chickens out and scratches the back of his neck.

His blue gaze digs deep into me, but I don't cower away. Growing up, I thought he'd always be by my side, but time has proven how... wrong we can be together. How volatile.

"Burying Jules...it killed me. And you weren't there," I croak.

"I'm sorry I abandoned you when you needed me the most."

After the funeral, Flynn disappeared inside a bottle. He numbed himself to the point of being unrecognizable, and I stopped believing in love altogether. He did reach out to me after a while, but by then I wanted nothing to do with him.

"I'm sorry I couldn't find a way to snap you out of it," I admit. "We have a tremendous task ahead of us. The hollows, the Unseelie—I don't want you to come with us if you won't take it seriously."

"If we have a shot at ending the war, I'm there. No booze. I promise. I want to help, whether or not this works out." He motions to the space between us.

I press my forehead to his. "Alright, Verinos. I'm in."

I cup his face and peck his lips, sealing my resolve to give us another chance. Jules is alive, and I'm ready to heal these wounds between us, one day at a time.

Jules lurks in the doorway, my shirt falling at her mid-thigh. "Everything okay?" She grins from ear to ear as though she heard everything.

As soon as she's within reach, I capture her in my arms and roll her between Flynn and me. She snuggles up to my side as Flynn buries his face in her neck, and I realize the weight dragging me down these past few years has simply...lifted. I'm not alone anymore. I don't have to protect my heart and my people without help.

I kiss the side of her head, drunk from her scent and love.

My partner in crime. My queen. My wife.

My Jules.

THE END… for now.

Lovely readers, thank you for this amazing journey. Now, we can embark on new adventures, starting with a return to the Shadow World in Princess of Thorns and Ruin.

Meet Arielle Delacroix, the vampire princess, as she navigates her new powers and the secrets and treachery of the Night Court.

This next reverse harem duet stands alone, but it is a direct continuation of the events in Magnetic, so if you haven't read that yet and you want to meet Vicky and her hot wolves, check it out **here**.

If you haven't read my free novella Hell over Heels featuring Kayde's twin brother, Lucas Barron, read here.

LOVELY READERS

*T*o support me and the books, please leave a rating or a review on Amazon.

THANK YOU FOR READING. I wrote Forbidden Magic after I fell in love with Holly Black's Cardan. If you haven't read her amazing series, *The Folks of The Air*, check it out.

I left a few threads hanging. I'm toying with the idea of writing two follow-up novels or novellas. The first would be from Allie's POV, where we get to explore her relationship with Barron. The second is the hunt for the Unseelie, where we could get more of my favorite trio and see their relationship evolve as they tear down the Unseelie with Mallory's help.

To keep up with my releases and receive exclusive extras, including bonus epilogues and special sneak peeks, join my newsletter.

Click here: http://bit.ly/anyaslair

Xoxo, Anya.

Connect with me on Facebook: https://www.facebook.com/AnyaJCosgrove/

Take a sneak peak at my completed witch trilogy after this.

SHADOW WALKER

*R*ead the series that started it all! Fall for the shadows. Kiss the enemy.

Nothing stays black and white in a world full of shadows...

I'm Alana Mitchell, and for my twentieth birthday, I got a brand-new magical destiny instead of the laptop I was saving for.

I'm a witch. I have powers I can't control, enemies I know nothing about, and a legacy I can't begin to grasp.

There's a shadow-world out there waiting to swallow me whole, a world I didn't even know existed until I used my magic and unleashed hell upon my naïve self. From heart-eating ghouls to glamors, potions, and spells... nothing is as it seems.

A renegade demon and his brother are teaching me the ropes and driving me crazy with their I-know-better attitudes, beckoning stares and stupidly handsome faces.

At this rate, I'll flunk Witchcraft 101. I want to hunt down the bastards that destroyed my future, but the brothers' past is threatening to steal my soul and tear me apart—literally.

To survive, I must embrace the darkness simmering inside me and unleash the devil within, no matter the consequences...

PICK UP YOUR COPY NOW!
  http://bit.ly/buyshadowwalker

MAGNETIC

Free on KU!

Who said life was a fairy tale? Because I'd gladly slice that jerk's head off.

I'm Vicky, though that's not really my name. Lying becomes second nature when you're on the run.

I never expected to end up half-naked in the woods. I didn't plan to stumble upon the most powerful shifter clan in North America and three of the sexiest men I've ever laid eyes on.

Dominic, the fun and reckless new wolf.

Sam, the hot doctor with glacial-blue eyes.

And Gabriel, the intense, secretive alpha who wants nothing to do with me.

My real name is a one-way ticket back to hell, and my secrets need to stay dead and buried like the girl I used to be.

Sleeping Beauty, Snow White, Red Riding Hood—I can be all three. I can use my powers to earn a place in their werewolf town, away from the bite of my past mistakes. I can use them—and their bodies—to survive.

The only thing I can't do is fall for them.

Magnetic is a stand-alone, steamy reverse harem romance featuring a kick-ass heroine and three swoon-worthy werewolves. Pick up your copy now!

www.ingramcontent.com/pod-product-compliance
Lightning Source LLC
Chambersburg PA
CBHW061134200626
46817CB00016B/1496